Praise for *Gathering of Angels: The Michael Saga Book 1*

"When I began reading Diana Henderson's latest novel, *Gathering of Angels*, the first in her series, *The Michael Saga*, I was instantly struck by the effortless flow of her writing style, character development, and captivating story. The more I entered the story, I found myself becoming deeply engaged, as though a distant soul memory was being re-activated. Not only is this great storytelling, but I feel changed spiritually after reading it. It contains profound teachings about faith, love, and healing from physical and emotional trauma. It also, most importantly, contains methods for anyone who feels that subtle pull to connect with their Angelic Team of Light. It is a story of deep love, both human and divine. This story is a healing balm for this age and for this moment that will raise the vibration and bring awareness and deeper understanding for anyone who is guided to read it." —Isabelle Dunnington, author of the *Twin Flames* series

"*The Michael Saga: Gathering of Angels* is one of those stories you will want to put down to save for tomorrow, but you can't. It will call to you to be part of the adventure. I loved gentle, relatable, and totally unassuming Michael and Melody. As they open to Archangel Michael and Metatron's presence and guidance, their purpose in the world transforms as does their love for one another. At times while reading this book, I felt as if I was receiving attunements from the archangels. The novel's lessons and truths are this powerful. Author Diana Henderson is an angelic treasure that we earthlings are blessed to have with us." —Sherrie Dillard, bestselling author of *I'm Still with You* and 10 other books translated into 12 languages

Gathering of Angels

The Michael Saga Book I

Gathering of Angels

The Michael Saga Book I

Diana Henderson

ISBN: 978-1-944662-67-7

Publishing date: July 2021

This is a work of fiction. Names, characters, businesses, places, events and incidents are either the products of the author's imagination or are used in a fictitious manner. Any resemblance to actual persons, living or dead, or actual events is purely coincidental. This book in no way seeks to represent a specific religion or spiritual practice. The author has no desire to interfere with any reader's personal beliefs.

Illustration by Zelenov Iurii purchased from Shutterstock.com.

Dedication

To all the angels in my life who have lifted me when I was in pain and stood by me through life's struggles and challenges

Acknowledgments

An abundance of thanks goes to Drew Becker, my husband, who has supported my writing and editing work for decades and who is my finest critic. Drew also serves as my editor and publisher.

Thank you to Worth Dewey Henderson, my late father, for being the consummate storyteller and to Doris Jarrett Henderson, my mother, for awakening and encouraging my love of books and writing.

I send much gratitude to the friends and family who have loved me and who have been my angels in human form by offering kindness, support, and wise counsel.

Thank you to the members of the Order of Archangel Michael and A Gathering of Angels who have attended my angel meetings and who believe in the grace of those unseen helpers in our lives.

Finally, I wish to thank Cheryl and Michael Penn, the owners of Tordown Bed & Breakfast, for allowing me to use their business and their names in this book. Their light shines through the pages of their website and the photos of their establishment, and I hope to one day visit this marvelous place in person.

Preface

> *"Angels transcend every religion, every philosophy, every creed. In fact, angels have no religion as we know it.... Their existence precedes every religious system that has existed on earth." —St. Thomas Aquinas*

I've believed angels were real for as long as I can remember and have found their presence altogether comforting in moments when my life hung on the precipice of destruction. As a teenager dealing with turbulent emotions and sometimes tragic circumstances, especially after six deaths of loved ones in six years, I placed myself in harm's way countless times. I could have died on any one of those occasions, but somehow, against all odds, I lived to tell the tales of an imagination that is deeply keyed into the spiritual worlds and the realms of angels and nature.

All my life, I've felt a kinship with the unseen. I've sensed a presence beyond this world and found myself drawn to explore those aspects of life that lie outside our mundane reality. That desire to peer into the realms of light has colored my life with wonder.

In this book, I invite you to consider what it would be like for angels to come to earth and live as humans, to forget their heavenly existence until the moment of their awakening when they would find each other and begin to live their purpose: rising beyond fear and into love.

Diana Henderson

Contents

Chapter One

The Tone

Translation of the Unspoken Tonal Language of Archangels

"I hold them all," he said to Metatron as he gazed down toward the earth.

"As do I."

Michael knew full well that his friend, companion, and brother enveloped all the earth. It was the way of an archangel. But he had served so long in proximity to humanity that the need to express seemed somehow natural.

"Divine law prevents us," Metatron said recognizing Michael's desire to intervene.

"Still, my kindred cry out to me as do yours," said Michael. "Their call enflames my heart."

"Yes, my fiery brother, and my mind is filled with the cries of each of my own, yet they knew the assignment and the risks."

"Knowing from here above it all and *living* as one of the humans, feeling the tremendous pain of separation—how could the 144,000 truly understand until they were in the midst of it? Sometimes it is more than my solar heart can bear, yet I will never turn away from them nor any soul on earth," Michael said.

"I may represent Creator's mind, my friend, but I perceive your meaning only too well. I am thankful that I was not birthed to the heart flame but to the creative intelligence. Still, every prayer and plea of humanity is woven into my psyche, and I was born to answer just as you were," Metatron replied.

"And what of she who is like your daughter and he who is as a son to me? I have held myself in oneness with them on occasion, and the feelings they endure.... I embrace their wounds for a span that I may lessen the pain for a moment. Would that I could do more," Michael said. The archangel's gaze blazed a swath of pure blue flame across the planet below.

Metatron placed his whirlwind of white light around Michael's flaming life force to lift and expand their energies of divine heart-mind. In doing so, he experienced the sensation of *feeling* as only the heart flame can.

"Ah, yes, I understand," Metatron said. "Perhaps it is time we made an appeal to Creator. It has been more than two of the earth's millennia since the last intercession."

"I am with you, my brother," said Michael. "The moment nears within the turning of the eternal. I feel the universal opening and shall rise home to stand before the throne."

"As one, we go then—the heart and the mind," Metatron replied. "To the throne, we are bound. Before the throne, we abide," Metatron intoned as his frequency began to expand into its galaxy-encompassing star tetrahedron. His vibration continued to shift upward, homeward. "I stretch into the mind, I Am!"

In exactly the same instant, Michael intoned, "I stretch into the heart, I Am!" His flames merged into Metatron's air-like whirlwind of pure light.

And the sound of a high-pitched hum was heard by every human on planet earth as the great opening to the center of creation invisibly anchored in the mind of all life.

* * *

Michael James Joseph Browne couldn't seem to get his ears to stop ringing. He had tried shaking his head, digging his little finger in his ear, even squirting water from an ear-cleaning bulb syringe that he purchased on his lunch break, and nothing helped. The sound was that of a high-pitched single note that played continuously for the last seven hours.

It wasn't unusual for Michael to experience the occasional hum. He heard those relatively often, but they usually only lasted a couple of minutes. Today, though, he was hoping he hadn't suddenly developed a case of severe tinnitus. The whine had started at exactly 11:11 a.m. He knew because he always glanced at the clock when he got one of these strange hums to see how long it would linger.

Lately they had become more frequent, and their duration had seemed to increase a bit as well. But it was after 6:00 now, and the noise was becoming a true annoyance as he navigated the rush hour traffic on his way home from work.

Sitting stuck amid an endless array of bumper-to-bumper vehicles wasn't exactly conducive to ignoring the sound, so after a while Michael tried recounting the ways his life had shifted in these last two years. First, he lost his job and went for a long while barely getting by on savings. His fiancée, who obviously was expecting more security from the relationship, left him and moved on. He spent lonely nights lacking sleep and days, weeks, and months searching for another position. His only comfort had been his retriever, Buddy, who had died three weeks before he started his new job. He sank into a depression after that but somehow managed to pick himself up and get through the learning curve with his current employer.

While these thoughts took his mind off the irritation of the loud tone, he didn't feel any better, so Michael tried to distract himself from the ringing by turning on the radio—just in time to hear an odd bit of news. The announcer on his favorite station happened to be talking about a loud hum in his ears that had been continuing since the late morning. He said he'd gotten calls all afternoon from people who shared the same experience. Many of them reported hearing these sounds sometimes but never to this extent or for this long.

"The phone here at the station has been ringing constantly—no pun intended—and this appears to be happening throughout the listening area here in Southern California. On that odd note, let's play an oldie by Santana to see if we can drown out the drone."

As "Smooth" started to play, Michael noticed the humming did not subside. Instead, it simply seemed to intermingle with the music as an irritating background to the melody. He was just about to cut off the radio when the announcer interrupted the track.

"Hold on, my friends," the man said. "I just got an update from our news director with wire service reports that verify this phenomenon is not only regional but nationwide and apparently worldwide. And get this: it appears that even the deaf are hearing the sound. I don't know what to say about that, folks, but people are speculating about everything from aliens to an international governmental conspiracy to the end of the world. Your guess is as good as mine at this point."

After a few more minutes of listening to sheer conjecture, Michael decided to turn off the radio. He thought back over his day and wondered at the fact that no one at work mentioned hearing the noise. But then his entire afternoon was spent in a team meeting with the project manager, who wasn't exactly the warmest person and had little tolerance for those who got off topic or off task. His droning, monotonous voice only added to the effect of the constant hum, producing a kind of absentminded and somewhat hypnotic haze. So that could explain the lack of sharing as well as the unresponsiveness of his coworkers when being asked for ideas and input on the project.

Over the coming days, Michael did his best to sleep, eat, work, and live with the sound. So did all the world for that matter. It was on the news 24-7 and took precedence over every other story. Some religious leaders believed it was the voice of God awakening humanity. There were a number of scientific theories including the idea that it was some sort of amplification of cosmic sound waves. One particularly poetic philosopher called it "the song of the universe opening the mind to infinite possibility."

Countless meetup groups sprang up across the country for people who wanted to discuss their ideas and experiences. A bit of a loner, Michael didn't feel drawn to attending any of these, but he did hear conversations at work and gathered that people's responses to the effect varied considerably. Some found it impossible to sleep, concentrate, or function while others, like him, somehow got used to the sound and even started to meditate to it. He found that he was able to go deep into theta brainwave state when he focused on the tone and dove into it. He experienced some strange visions as a result—geometric forms made of energy, massive pillars of white light and blue flame, and other scenes he didn't really understand.

Just as the hum was starting to become simply another part of the background of life for most people, it suddenly stopped—exactly 44 days to the minute from when it began.

* * *

Melody's art career hadn't exactly been flourishing. She had moved to Venice Beach in hopes of finding inspiration, but little fueled her creative flow with the exception of the daily sunsets over the ocean. The sky and sea blending into their myriad of rainbow hues washed her inner being at the close of every day. She'd sold a few drawings and paintings here and there but made more on her portraits of passersby. She had to wait tables to manage the rent and have at least a meal a day to keep her nourished.

But the strangest thing happened at the onset of the hum that became the background of everyone's lives on that morning that enlivened the world. Since then, all she could seem to paint were angels with shapes and symbols she didn't fully comprehend. Geometry was her least favorite subject in high school, but here she was painting octahedrons and tetrahedrons and some forms whose names she couldn't recall behind large glowing angels. For the whole 44 days of the hum, her every spare moment from waking to sleep was filled with the vision of these beautiful beings. Sometimes she painted them in soft pastels or watercolors with the lightest touch she could manage. Others required a heavier hand and oils that allowed her to work the image until it molded to the vision in her mind.

Every morning she awakened with yet another picture in her head—often more than one—and she sketched each image quickly so they would not be lost in the mad rush to bring them all to life. She felt somehow that if she completed all the paintings, shared every image, that in some bizarre way it might change the world. She kept this notion to herself and knew how perfectly crazy it sounded. On occasion, she considered that the constant ringing in her ears was simply driving her mad. She hoped she wouldn't be cutting off an ear anytime soon. Van Gogh she was not, of course, but his use of color, his vivid, inimitable style spoke to her deeply, and, although she would never imagine aspiring to his genius, she sometimes dreamed of touching the heart as purely as his work did.

Since the sound influx, she also started going to a local gathering twice a week to meet people who were affected by the hum. She hoped to find someone else who had received increased creativity or imagery, but so far no one she encountered had that sort of reaction. After a while she started to venture farther from home to attend one group after another in search of a single person who shared what she was experiencing. But not a soul seemed able to relate to what was now her life.

Melody had planned to attend a meeting in L.A. that was scheduled on the night the world sound stopped. The drive would take almost an hour, and she strongly considered not going. But she kept feeling a pull, a strange urgency that almost begged her to make the trip. So she listened to her heart and headed into Los Angeles.

* * *

Michael couldn't believe he was doing this. The entire 44 days he somehow managed to avoid seeking answers by visiting the groups that literally could be found in almost every community. But tonight, after several hours without the hum, he felt a little adrift. It was as though the sound had anchored him in some profound way that he didn't recognize until it was absent. Now an overwhelming desire to connect to that hum led him to find a local meeting and sign up to attend.

As he walked in the door and surveyed the room, he saw only a few people huddled near the front of the space. They appeared to be well acquainted—no doubt regulars. Off to the left on her own, a woman with long, straight blonde hair sat, appearing slightly uneasy and out of place. *First-timer like me*, he thought. As he glanced in her direction, she turned around and gazed straight at him, her eyes meeting his with a look of recognition. Had he met her somewhere before? He sifted through memories and determined he had not, but he felt as though he knew her.

Walking directly up to her was not his style at all, but his feet were doing exactly that. "Hi," he said. "I'm Michael Browne. It's my first time here."

"Hi, Michael. I'm Melody Childress. Mine too." She smiled as someone does when greeting an old friend.

"We haven't met before, have we?" he asked still feeling that sense of recognition.

"No. I mean, I don't know. You seem somehow very familiar to me. I'm sure we haven't met, but I feel like we have." She sighed like a person who is used to not being understood. "I know that doesn't make much sense," she added.

Words escaped his mouth without the usual filter he employed when meeting new people. "I get exactly what you're saying," he told her. "I'm feeling a little lost today since the sound stopped. I know lots of people are happy about it, but I'm not. It's hard to describe what it did for me, but I can tell you that I will miss it."

"So will I," she said. "Listen, I haven't found anybody else who has had my experience. Maybe you'll understand. Maybe you won't. I don't know. Here's the thing…"

She paused, holding her breath for a moment, then inhaling deeply before saying in one long outbreath, "I've been having visions of angels and geometric forms and lots of wild and beautiful things, and I don't want to lose that."

She looked at him with eyes that hoped.

"Yes," he said. "That's it exactly. A few days in, I started to meditate with the hum, to move into it instead of away from it, and I saw things…well…indescribably beautiful shapes and colors and, yes, geometric forms!"

The expression on her face and light in her eyes spoke volumes as she listened to him. His heart suddenly felt like it was on fire—like he might spontaneously combust at any moment. A kind of electricity started to pass between them. He couldn't explain what was happening. Was he going to pass out?

Then her gaze seemed to move through him as if she were seeing something at a great distance, and she began to speak again.

"Heart of flame," she whispered. "Blue flame who shares the name." Then she appeared to be jolted back to reality.

"What just happened?" he said.

"I had one of my visions, but it was of you…and somehow more than you. I don't know really. I just saw you as this massive pillar of blue flame with wings of fire spreading out around you. It was you but more than you…. Please don't run off and think I'm just crazy. Unless, of course, I am. Who knows at this point," she added with an awkward half-smile.

"If you're crazy, then I guess I am too," he replied. "I felt your words like a fire inside my heart. Look, I don't say things like this. I don't understand what's happening to me."

"Whatever it is, we're both a part of it," she said. "I think maybe we need to leave. It looks like they're about to start the meeting, and I don't think I can sit through it. I need to walk on the beach and feel the sand under my feet."

"That sounds about like heaven to me," he said. "I feel stranger than I have in my whole life, and frankly that's saying a lot for someone who never thought I belonged." Again, the truth simply slipped from his lips without restraint.

Without thinking about getting up for work the next day or much of anything else, at her invitation he got in his car and followed her home to Venice Beach. It was a good 50 minutes from his place, but he knew he had to be there and to walk beside her.

By the time they reached their destination, the summer sun hung low over the ocean as the day neared its end. The two of them walked together beside the Pacific. Although the beach was filled with the usual array of people seeking the blazing sunset view, he knew they were alone there in a real sense, alone among a crowd somehow set apart from the *real world*.

"Maybe we're not from here," she said as they sat on the sand, eyes turned toward the luminous sky streaked in hues of violet, peach and gold. The vastness of the sea and sky made him feel small.

"But at the same time infinite," she whispered as though his thoughts had been voiced aloud. She turned to him, seemingly unaware she had just read his mind.

"I was thinking how the ocean and the sky made me feel small," he replied, "and my next thought was 'but also infinite,' and that's exactly what you said. Were you hearing my thoughts?" He was both unnerved and yet totally okay with the idea.

"Are you sure you didn't say it out loud?" she asked. "I would have sworn I heard you say those words."

"I promise I was only thinking them."

"That's pretty weird, huh?" She turned toward him as if peeling her eyes away from the view was almost painful.

"You know what's even stranger?" he asked. "I *feel* you. Let me rephrase that," he added with a smile. "Just then I thought I felt that you didn't want to look away from the ocean, like somehow this view was almost like…I don't know. The only thing that comes to mind is…*home*." He realized the emphasis on the last word was stronger than he meant it to be. He'd always longed for everything that word conjured in his mind and heart but never quite found it.

She smiled. "That is exactly what I was feeling. *Home*. But not back in my hometown. Not anywhere I've found except that endless sky and boundless sea filled with the colors of my heart." She laughed slightly. "I didn't mean to sound so… poetic."

He noticed that her clear blue eyes had a darker, almost cobalt circle around their outer edge. It was odd, he thought. The only time he'd seen eyes like those were when he looked into the mirror. He had a moment of wondering if they were related, but where he was tan and dark-haired she was pale and blonde. Still, he found it interesting that her eyes so resembled his own.

"What do you think is happening with all this—your reading my thoughts and me sensing your feelings—if that's what we're doing?"

She didn't blink as she said, "I think we were meant to find each other today. I had never been to that meeting or any of them that far away from here, and I felt *compelled* to go, and it had to be that *exact* place."

"I hadn't been to a single meeting up to this point," he replied, "and I felt I *had* to be there too."

"You noticed our eyes, didn't you?" she asked. "We look like twin children of a different mother and father." She smiled and so did he.

"Since we're just laying things out without any pretense, I think I should tell you that I feel we might be related but not necessarily in the usual sense," he said, surprising himself.

She stared past him again as if gazing beyond this world into the next. Her expression was peaceful. Some kind of inner knowing led him to be still and close his eyes. He breathed more slowly and attempted to evoke the sound of the hum that had filled his mind for the last 44 days. As he did, he found himself again able to tune in to her feelings. He sensed something he had never experienced. He could only call it *bliss*.

Michael wondered if he could pick up on her thoughts too, so he tried opening his mind, which soon became flooded with brilliant blue light spiraling and dancing inside his head. Within the cobalt background, white shapes began to form—glowing orbs and what he could only describe as crystallized flower designs repeated and overlapping. Then, it seemed that every geometric shape he ever learned revealed itself one after another moving into a larger figure.

"Metatron's cube," he whispered. *Where did that come from?* He must have heard it somewhere. Now he remembered. His ex-fiancée had a necklace that he had found beautiful. She used that term to describe it.

As he opened his eyes, Melody was looking at him. "Metatron," she said. "I heard you say 'Metatron.'"

"Yes, I was seeing these glowing white designs take shape again on an electric blue background, and I remembered what it was from a necklace someone in my past wore."

"You were seeing my vision," she said, half question, half statement. "You're describing what I saw. Did you hear the sound too? Not as loud as before, but it was there."

Michael realized that he had. He had begun trying to evoke the tone inwardly, but somewhere along the way he actually just allowed it to come. And it did.

A tingle went up his spine that shook his torso, and he noticed she mirrored the movement in the same moment.

"Wow," she said. "I felt the biggest zing go up my spine, and it looks like you did too."

He simply nodded. A hundred thoughts rushed through his mind at the speed of light—all focused on one thing: *What does this mean? What's happening to us?*

Melody stood and reached down her hand for his. "I've got to show you something," she said. "Or several somethings."

The sky was deepening and the last rays of setting sunlight ushered them along the shore.

"My place is a few blocks from here," she said. "I never invite people back there, but I know you have to see my art."

They walked together to her apartment. On entering, the first thing he noticed was that there were no frills—just simple midcentury modern furniture and very little else except on the walls, which were filled with paintings of sunsets that echoed the real thing but with something more—an ethereal glow that made them seem almost otherworldly.

"Is this your art?" he asked. "I'm so glad you decided to show me these. They're amazing."

"Thank you," she said, "but that's not what I meant."

She guided him to a corner where canvases and sketch pads leaned against a wall. Clearly, she was prolific given the number of canvases. One by one, she revealed paintings reminiscent of the vision he had seen on the beach and the many images that came to him during the "hum meditations." But these had something more: angels, angels, and more angels.

"I can't believe these," he said in a low tone. "These are just like my meditation images, but you've added angels to them. I've got to tell you, I think these are the most perfect paintings I've ever seen."

She beamed at the compliment. Literally. He was gazing at her against the one blank wall in her space, and he would have sworn he saw a white light expand around her head and shoulders. *I must really be going off the deep end*, he thought.

She laughed then. “We’re diving into the same end of the pool,” she said. “Or the deepest part of the ocean, I think.”

Michael wondered for a split second if he could be having a dream. This beautiful girl, her art, their meeting, the mind-reading and shared feelings—was it all just some strange but entirely wonderful dream? If so, he wasn’t sure he wanted to wake up.

“The hum,” said Melody. “It woke me up. I feel in a way that I never *lived* until that day. Like I was just going through the motions and waiting for something. I just didn’t know what.”

He was about to reply when the door opened and a tall, slender young woman walked in. The moment she entered, Michael felt as if some kind of spell had been broken. But more than that, he sensed a shadow fall over the space. He always had this uncanny ability to get impressions of people’s vibes or mood, and he took an instant dislike to this person.

“This is my roommate, Casey. Casey, this is Michael Browne. I met him tonight at the meeting.”

“Hi. Nice to meet you. Look, I’m not much into company right now. I didn’t get the commercial I auditioned for this morning, and I’ve had a long shift on my feet at the restaurant. So excuse me for being antisocial, but I’ve got to get some sleep and get ready for another audition tomorrow.”

Without a backward glance, she left the room, went down the hall, and closed a door behind her near the end of the corridor.

“I guess that’s my cue to exit,” Michael said. But he could still sense the energy coming from the room down the hall and from the person inside it. This didn't feel like just a bad mood to him. He knew he wanted to get far away from that shadow as quickly as possible, but he also had a strong desire to somehow shelter Melody from it.

Without a filter or a thought, he quietly said, "Melody, you need to get a different roommate." He could hardly believe those words came out of his mouth.

Her soothing smile evoked even more intense feelings of wanting to protect her.

"Oh, Casey's all right. She's just in a bad mood. I would be too with that kind of day. She was counting on that commercial."

Michael looked intently into her eyes and spoke softly. "No, she really isn't *all right*, Melody. I know we just met and I have no concrete reason to say this, but I sense something I can't explain. It's a feeling I've had before and it's always, *always* been right." Looking back toward the hallway, in almost a whisper, he added, "There's something *wrong* there, something really wrong."

Melody appeared hurt, which was the last thing he wanted to do. She gazed down and away from him.

"Look," he said, "you've known me for all of two hours. But if you come outside with me back onto the beach, I think I can help you understand."

She appeared unsure but agreed, and they walked outside together as far as he felt they needed to go. Slipping out of their shoes, they went out into the ocean up to their ankles before he knew it was *safe* to talk.

"This is new to me," he said. "I've never put words to this sort of thing before. But maybe we can just breathe together and feel the water and sand on our feet and see what happens."

They stood there facing each other, inhaling and exhaling in unison. The crowd of passersby on the strand seemed to fade and become far away, and the sound of the ocean began to hum inside their minds. Michael closed his eyes and opened his heart and mind. He realized suddenly that he'd never exposed his inner being to anyone so much in his entire life—not his younger brothers, his parents, his former fiancée, *no one*. But that didn't stop him. He let her into every part of himself, his life, his being. He leveled all the walls of a lifetime in a single moment to invite in this beautiful woman whom he somehow trusted. And then he simply thought of the moment Casey had entered the space.

Something occurred beyond his experience then. In his mind's eye, he really *saw* a kind of murky energy surrounding her and a dark figure hovering over her. He could hardly believe this was happening. He'd sensed what he thought of as bad vibes many times but never perceived anything like this.

Melody gasped and drew back suddenly. "God, what was that?" she said.

"I don't know," he replied. "But that's what I was feeling and why I said you should find a new roommate."

He could hear sadness in her voice as she responded. "She's not just my roommate; we work together at the same restaurant. She helped me get the job, and, although most of the restored furniture is mine, I'm the one renting space from her. I don't have any place else to go."

"Yes, you do," he said. "You can stay with me—at least for tonight. I'll take the couch and you can have the bedroom. If you don't mind a bit of a mess, you can just follow me home, and we'll figure things out tomorrow."

It didn't matter that they just met tonight. He knew her better than anyone he'd encountered in as long as he could remember. He hoped and sensed she felt the same.

"All right," she said. "Let's go back so I can get my keys and a few things I'll need. This is maybe the craziest thing I've ever done, you know. But I would trust you with my life," she said looking up at him in the dimness.

He felt the fire in his chest again spreading into every particle of his being. An endless stream of questions echoed through his mind now, but he knew the answers would all be found in one place: his heart.

Chapter Two

The Light and the Shadow

Michael, the archangel, spread his blazing light into the Father's heart. Here is where he lived always in the eternal essence of Creator. Although there could be no sense of separation from that which one is, the return to the throne, the letting go and merging totally into the pure core of home, the deepest union of being with that which is all, was sheer ecstasy.

"Beloved Father, *I Am*," he intoned as a single note of pure heart fire. And all that his own heart held was known in an instant and became a part of the light stream of creation.

Metatron lived forever in this place and yet also served in an infinite number of others in the eternal moment that is creation. He was ever here and always there. Still, the return to the throne, to the center of pure divine mind filled him with the quintessence of bliss.

"Beloved Creator, *I Am*," he sang, and his every prayer, intention, and thought were woven into the oneness of the white light.

In less than a wink of the all-seeing eye, the two leaders of the archangels expressed and experienced every thought, feeling, and potential outcome. The light streams of eternity for every soul on earth revealed themselves in the infinity of possibility. Both Michael and Metatron exuded the epitome of gratitude for the dispensation granted. Michael's heart of pure flame flowed love unending while Metatron's mind emanated its melody of thanks.

With their assignments clear and the knowing of what must be done enmeshed into every particle of their beings, the two archangels departed through the cosmic doorway and returned to their posts above the planet earth.

* * *

As he drove back to his place, Michael kept an eye in the rearview mirror to be sure she was still following him and hadn't gotten blocked in traffic. He was still trying to come to grips with everything he had experienced during this bizarre evening that, if scripted, could never be believed. Although he wasn't in the movie industry, it was impossible to live in L.A. and not think in those terms. It would make for an outlandish script to be sure, but these days that seemed to be what people watched.

Michael's tastes tended to run toward drama and dramatic fantasy. Since the onset of the hum and especially his meeting with Melody tonight, it seemed his life had taken a turn toward the latter.

He knew that when he got home, he'd find a sink full of dishes, an unmade bed, clothes scattered around the bedroom, and even a few draped over the couch if he recalled correctly. At least he had warned her it would be a mess. As he pulled into the apartment complex and parked in front of his tiny flat, he decided to focus on what was way more important than his being a slob.

Michael motioned for Melody to park next to him in one of the two spaces that came with his place. He had paid the extra for another spot before his fiancée left him and rarely used it now except if his parents or his brother Tom came in from the northern part of the state to visit.

Melody followed him into his apartment and patiently waited by the door while he picked up a few things so she could sit.

"Sorry about the mess," he said. "Your place was so neat and tidy and now you have to come into this."

"Don't worry. I've got a younger sister who was never what you'd call neat," she said with an understanding smile. "I can help you tidy things a bit if you want," she added.

"Thanks, but no. My feeling is if you mess it up, you clean it. It's just how I am. I'll put some fresh sheets on the bed later and clear things away before you go to sleep. Don't worry."

"You don't need to do anything special. I can handle things just the way they are."

"Well, maybe so, but I'd like to make you comfortable." He genuinely meant that. Now that she was here, he actually felt the place was more like home than it had ever been.

She looked into his eyes and said, "Thank you." He wasn't sure whether she was reading his mind again or just responding to his words. Those mirror eyes of hers expressed only kindness. When he gazed into them, it felt like the path to home lay just beyond those clear blue irises rimmed in cobalt.

"I wish we'd met sooner," she said. "I love my friends, but I've always felt alone—until tonight."

The fire in his chest expanded again its blue-white heat, and he wondered if he was going to keel over.

"Are you all right?" she asked.

"I'm fine," he said. "It's just that I've had the strangest sensation several times tonight—a kind of fire in my heart. But I don't mean heartburn or anything like that. Honestly, it feels like some kind of furnace turning on and blazing heat. Frankly, it feels similar to how my mother describes her hot flashes," he added with a laugh.

"I'm feeling something too but different from that," she said. "I keep having this sensation that my head is about 10 times its normal size and that I'm really, really expansive. It's been making me a little lightheaded to be honest. I was fine in the car the whole way here, but now that we're in the same room, I started sensing that again. I feel almost like a part of me is very, very tall, like I'm here but I'm also up there." She pointed toward the ceiling.

"We're quite a pair," he said. Then, his heart spoke again without any interference from his mind. "I believe we're kin, and I've known you forever."

She reached out her hand, and he met hers with his own, his right hand covering her left. Electricity ran between them. He could feel it flowing through him into her. Then she extended her right palm over his left, and he sensed a flood of energy moving up his arm straight to his heart.

Tears began to flow down her cheeks or was it down his own? No, he thought, it had to be both. And the only word resounding through his brain, his body, his being was home. Home. *Home.*

He pulled his hands apart from hers and embraced her as though she were his long-lost beloved. Overwhelmed with emotion, he let every hope of his life, every dream of something more that he dared not truly believe, pour from his being.

"Michael," she said. She repeated the name over and over again as though intoning or chanting as a mantra. "At last," she whispered softly.

After what could have been two minutes or an hour or a lifetime, she pulled away and peered again into his eyes. Her face was still etched in wet streaks.

"I didn't realize I'd waited all my life for this moment," she said. "If you knew how hard it had been, how alone I've felt…."

"I do," he replied. "I never fit, you know. Until now, that is. When I started to meditate to the hum and to see those shapes and colors in my head, I finally began to feel more at ease in the world, but this is so far beyond that."

"For me, I've only ever felt at home in my art, especially the paintings I've been doing for the last 44 days. Any time away from that seemed pale and lacking any sense of reality, but now I feel I've found… I don't even know the words."

For a long while, they just sat there silently searching the depths of each other's eyes. Finally, he realized that it was getting late, and he would need to get up early, so he cleared off the bed, changed the sheets, and tried to make the bedroom a little more inviting for his guest. They said goodnight with an embrace that sent electric shocks through his entire system. Before he fell asleep, with more meaning and truth than in any moment of his life, he whispered, "Thank you, God. Thank you."

* * *

Michael had experienced unusual, vivid dreams for much of his life. Since he was a small child, in the realm of the unconscious, he had met all kinds of interesting beings and had conversations with people he had never met in waking life as well as the occasional visit from his late grandfather. He always supposed these were the product of an active subconscious and too many farfetched movies and books.

Although the lucid quality was common enough, tonight's dream was like no other before it. An impossibly tall man stood over Michael. Around his shoulders wings of blue fire expanded far beyond the ceiling. His eyes glowed with the same flame that appeared to blaze behind them, and around his head shone a solar corona so bright it was almost as blinding as the sun on a clear day. The winged giant reached out a hand and wordlessly spoke into his mind, "Come, Michael."

Michael took the hand without question and was transported instantly to another place. Large buildings appeared to be made of white light nearby, but they walked into a garden that was like nothing on earth. Trees loomed higher than the canopy of white clouds above, and flowers bloomed in colors unseen by human eye.

Again, the great being seemed to sound words inside his mind without giving voice. In the background Michael noticed a high-pitched and by now familiar hum.

"This time, you will remember, my old friend," the being said. "We've shared these journeys during your sleep many times, but I have allowed you the luxury of not recalling until this moment was at hand."

Michael's human mind could not imagine forgetting any meeting with this great being. He stood beside this massive presence in awe of the commanding quality of his every expression.

"I am Michael," the giant said. "You know me as Archangel Michael, but I exist across the ages and the infinite dimensions known by only the tone or signature of my light. You bear my name in this life as do many of my kindred on earth. You also bear my gifts, and one of these is finally quickening in your waking consciousness. What you saw and sensed on this very evening was only the beginning.

"You need to be prepared now. You have found the way to open your solar heart to the flames that are our essence, but you will need to remember how to once again wield the sword of light and wear the shield of protection at its fullest intention."

Michael Browne felt as if these words were being emblazoned on his psyche by the archangel's powerful energy.

"You do not recall it yet, but you are my lieutenant and as dear to me as a son. I have watched over you in every moment of your human existence and shall continue."

Michael was dumbstruck by the flood of knowing entering into his mind. He could hardly process what Archangel Michael was saying to him. How could he be what this magnificent angel said? He was just an ordinary human being, yet he knew the truth even as he recognized the light shining so brilliantly with every word intoned into his consciousness.

"You were among the 144,000 sent to earth to be present for the great awakening and the span of shadow before the age of light," Archangel Michael continued. "You must be on guard now and more vigilant than ever because that moment is upon you. You have always been able to sense the shadow. Now you must be aware of its movements and machinations and avoid the traps into which so many of humanity have fallen prey.

"Are you ready to remember?" the archangel asked.

"Yes," Michael said. In truth, he could only hope so, but somehow he knew that in all his existence he never had nor ever would say "no" to Archangel Michael.

The great archangel reached out his right hand and placed it on Michael's forehead. Instantly, Michael's awareness expanded and he began to see worlds of light, realms beyond imagining, the heart of creation itself blazing its infinite fuel for all life. His view then turned toward the earth, and he perceived a shadow covering the world, a great light constantly flooding it, breaking through, clearing it, and more shadow forming as if it rose from the planet.

"Human miscreation," Archangel Michael said. "What you discern is the hatred, anger, pity, aggression, greed, and discord of humanity. The view you are seeing is from six months past as humans measure time. Humans are not only fueling but creating more entities and energies for us to cleanse, but the law of free will prevents us from intervening in many cases."

Viewing the scene, Michael found it daunting. How could so much gloom ever be cleared?

"It can and it will," Archangel Michael said. "Now I will reveal what occurred over the last 44 of your days."

Michael watched as a great wave of light spread across the entire planet and grew in intensity. Then the shadows gradually started reappearing and expanding especially around certain parts of the world.

"Today, as the Metatron wave ceased its activity, humanity already began reformulating the old pattern. My brother Metatron and I along with many others of our kindred are working to clear the pattern itself, but it is deeply ingrained into certain parts of the world where wars and hate have so long held sway. Beyond this, humanity has already set in motion so many programs of judgment and disharmony, and each one of you chooses the light or the shadow in every moment. Either choice determines the energies that fill and surround your being as you move through the world."

As Michael digested these truths, a profound sense of responsibility filled him.

"My old friend," said Archangel Michael, "you have always known this in your heart, have you not?"

Gazing into the giant angel's flaming blue eyes, Michael nodded.

"This is only part of why you journeyed with me tonight. I am calling you to the task for which you came to earth," Archangel Michael said. "Will you again wield with me the sword of light?"

An intense, fiery stirring burned in Michael's heart as he agreed. No other answer was possible. He knew this in every fiber of his being.

In that moment, the archangel's appearance altered as his immense being transformed into a blazing pillar of blue flame that moved to encompass Michael. He felt tiny contained within that enormous column of fire. But swiftly his own consciousness seemed to stretch into the warm, reassuring flames and experience them as his true nature. He sensed the blue-white blaze reaching deep into his being to an inner core where the living sword of light had been held in waiting for this moment. He felt it awaken and instantly ignite. A knowing passed through him as visions flooded his consciousness of ages spent in service to the cause of protecting the innocent and cleansing the shadow—back to back and side by side with his teacher, his friend, the keeper of the great sword formed of the purest love in existence. The past, present, and future all seemed to blend into one as together they stood outside time.

The blue flames of the pillar began to saturate his cells. He knew this was perception on his part but was also aware that the actuality of the experience was happening in his body, which lay sleeping so far from this place of light. He saw an octahedron and a sphere forming from the flames to house his human self.

"Your shield," said the archangel in an utterance that permeated the whole of Michael's awareness.

When the awakening was complete, the fiery column moved away from him, and once again he took on his previous appearance.

"You will know what to do and when to take action," Archangel Michael said. "The divine laws have been recorded upon your human mind as well, and it is vital to live by them. I must warn you to avoid judgment at all costs, for your shield cannot function ideally while you exist in the state of judging.

"Be aware that you will sense and sometimes see the shadow. It is vital to look away as rapidly as you can so that it cannot connect to you. Gaze always toward the Light, for therein lies your strength and the source of all power.

"And protect her. She is not equipped in the same way you are. Creator angels, which is her soul's truth, know only light. Although she has experienced many wounds during her human experience, her power is the act of creation itself, and her only protection is the innocence and purity of her heart. She cannot dwell long upon the shadow without losing some of that purity.

"I must return you to the body now, but I will see you again. Your work now is to remember as you are willing and ready, to pay attention always, to guard your thoughts, words, and actions. And one final thing. This you will remember and act upon: You are to travel to Glastonbury Tor and climb to St. Michael's Tower in the darkest time of the year. Be there on your birthday. And take her with you. Despite the cold and damp of December, know that you will be sheltered, and you will not be alone."

Back in his body, Michael awakened with a start. He peered into the dark space to see if he could view the clock on the microwave. It read 4:44. He thought he heard Melody stirring in the bedroom and went to tap lightly on the door.

"Michael," she said softly. "It's okay. Come in."

She had turned on the lamp next to the bed and sat up looking radiant and beautiful even in the dim light. "I just had the most amazing experience of my life," she said. "I met Metatron!"

Chapter Three

Archangel Encounters

After discussing their experiences, Michael and Melody realized that they had similar encounters. Melody had gone to a sanctuary that appeared rather like a crystal palace of pure white light. She saw many of the images from her paintings come to life—geometric forms etched out of crystalline light floating in the air.

"And he let me gaze into eternity," she said. That's the only way I can describe it. I could never put into words what I experienced."

"It was the same for me. Worlds and dimensions overlapping and expanding infinitely."

"Did Archangel Michael tell you what to do next?" she asked.

"He said I had to be on guard and *never* to judge, and he wants me to protect you." Michael looked into her eyes and knew he would gladly do that with every ounce of strength he could muster.

She smiled at him. "That's interesting," she said. "Metatron told me to protect you. He said you'd need me to remind you that the world was more than cruelty and destruction, that there was always love and light and always, always to look toward it."

"Archangel Michael said something about that too. It's been so easy these last few years to see all the horrible things in the world and hard to find the good. That changed with the hum though. I sort of got back to being more me."

He didn't quite know what that meant anymore. Tonight had transformed everything, yet he was still the same in some ways. He was still Michael.

"Michael, my body is vibrating. It's sort of tingling all over. Do you feel that way?" Melody asked.

"Yes, it's like my cells are firing constantly and almost like I can feel the atoms in my body moving super fast. I think it's getting a little less intense the longer we talk."

He gazed at the bedside clock and saw that it was already 5:30 in the morning. They had talked for over 90 minutes, and he had to be up in less than an hour. At this point it didn't make sense to try and squeeze in more sleep, so the two of them sat on the bed continuing to compare their journeys.

"Oh, I almost forgot," he said. "I have to book a flight to England. It's months away, but I feel the need to do it now."

"Can you make that tickets for two? I can pay you back if you don't mind waiting for a while until I sell another few paintings."

"Don't worry," said Michael. "I've got this."

Michael booked two tickets from LAX to Bristol Airport leaving on December 3, three days before his birthday—enough time to get to Glastonbury and visit St. Michael's Tower on the appointed date. He realized it would take him a long while to pay off the credit card bills for the trip, but he didn't think twice about doing what had to be done.

"Michael, I will pay you back for mine," she said.

"Melody, I want to do this. I feel…I don't know…like I wouldn't want to go without you by my side."

She smiled again in that knowing way as if she were sensing exactly what he felt. "All right…for now."

"We've got more pressing concerns right now anyway," he said. "I think you're going to need to move out of your place as soon as possible. Truth is I don't even want you going back there."

"I've got to go back. I need to give Casey some kind of notice. It's almost the end of the month, so it wouldn't be right to not pay for August."

He sensed her genuine concern and felt the battle raging inside her over what to do. "I see only one solution then unless you've got a better one. You can stay here. I know it won't be convenient to where you work, but you can stay here rent free until you find another place, and you and I can continue to explore our understanding of all this."

"I don't want you to have to sleep on the sofa for a month, and I won't be able to afford another place for at least that long."

"I'll get an air mattress if I need to. It will be fine. Besides my couch is pretty comfy. I fall asleep on it often enough as it is." He grinned at her. "Don't you see how perfect this will be?"

He had the most intense feeling that someone was standing over his shoulder nodding in approval. To confirm that, she started gazing beyond him again as if seeing what he could not.

"Yes," she said. "I do see now. I guess sometimes I have to be reminded to accept help when it's offered. Thank you."

It seemed as though a great weight had been lifted from them both. He realized that he had been feeling her emotions and concerns as if they were his. As she let them go, he sensed the shift in her as though it were his own.

They made plans to get her things, especially her art. She decided she would leave the furniture at the apartment with Casey until she moved fully *if* her soon-to-be former roommate would agree.

"I have a shift at the restaurant from 3 to 11 today and wouldn't be able to be back here until midnight," she said.

"I have an extra key I'll give you. In the meantime, I need to get ready for work, and maybe you should get some more sleep," he said with a smile.

As he rose from the bed, she reached out and touched his forearm. "You don't know how much this means to me," she said.

An overwhelming sense of relief and gratitude filled his inner being. "Oh, I think I do," he said. "Still feeling what you feel, after all. It's going to be an interesting time."

* * *

Melody heard Michael leave as she drifted back off. As she glided effortlessly into that floating state between waking and sleeping, the visions began again. Her inner awareness stretched into the vastness of the cosmos where worlds were being born, stars were dying, and the infinite act of creation was taking place in every moment. Deeper into the vision, she perceived glowing orbs, crystalline shapes, and geometric forms in some great dance that perpetually expanded the light of life.

There she sensed his presence, Metatron, whom she had known forever and only now remembered. She was not whisked away as before; she merely soared in the space of knowing, of sensing what existed beyond the edge of perception. Here her next painting came to her. She saw it as clearly as if she were looking at the finished canvas. As always, the tone of light sounded in her mind like some pure resonance of the spirit. So sweetly the song of creation played.

She had the thought that she should get up and sketch the image to avoid losing it, but a voice out of the ethers spoke into her thoughts, "All is well. Sleep now. You will recall it perfectly upon awakening." And so she sank deeply into the stillness.

When she came back to consciousness, it took a moment to realize where she was. She thought back on the last 16 hours and marveled at everything that had transpired. While her life had changed significantly when the hum began, she now realized that was just the beginning of a journey she could never have imagined.

Rousing from deep slumber, she prepared for the day. Michael had been so kind. He even thought to leave a fresh towel for her with a note that she could use the shower or anything else she needed. She felt closer to this man whom she had known for less than a day than to anyone in the world.

She found that the next image for her art was etched upon her mind to such a degree that she didn't feel the need to sketch it immediately, which was good since she didn't have her materials, and there wouldn't be time once she went back to her place.

The day moved more swiftly than usual, it seemed. On her ride home, she memorized the route exactly. Even with GPS on her phone, she liked to note the landmarks along the way.

She didn't see her roommate on her arrival and assumed Casey was either at the beach or had another audition that afternoon. She was thankful not to face her just yet. After dressing for work, she pulled together all that she would need for that night and the next day, including her sketch pad and her pastel pencils. She left a note for Casey explaining that she would be out again and return the next day. She couldn't break the news of her impending and sudden move in a note.

Since this was Casey's day off at the restaurant, she felt more at ease on her way there. As she drove to work, she had a soothing sense of being watched over and a kind of inner knowing that this would go more smoothly if she didn't worry about it. So for once she listened and actually let go of her concerns about what that meeting with her roommate would be like.

As she pulled into the restaurant parking lot, she spotted Casey's car. She must have taken another shift or be filling in for someone. Feelings of panic started to rise in Melody's chest, but then a sense of stillness seemed to overtake her anxiety, and she knew she was not alone in this.

It wasn't until their break that Melody had a chance to talk with her roommate.

"Where were you last night?" she said. "I came out of my room and you were just *gone*. Please don't tell me you went home with that guy you just met."

"Actually, I did," Melody replied. "But it wasn't like that. He and I *connected*—just not in the way you're thinking."

A sudden inner caution came to her, and she knew she had to be careful with her words and avoid talking about anything substantive regarding Michael, the angels, the entire experience.

"Listen, I know this is sudden and you'll think I'm crazy, but I'm going to be moving to his place. Please don't worry though. I'll pay for next month's rent, and that should give you plenty of time to find someone else to move in."

"Are you totally *insane*?" Casey asked. "You just met this guy last night, right? And now you're telling me you're going to move in with him?"

"Like I said, I know how strange it sounds. It just feels absolutely right to me."

She couldn't say that she was only going to stay with Michael until she found another living space. That would open the door for too many questions. Better that Casey should think her foolish than to wonder why she would suddenly leave their apartment for no apparent reason.

"Is it all right if I leave my furniture for a while? I won't need it at Michael's, but I could put it into storage if you want. Obviously, I will get all my paintings and art supplies."

Casey appeared to be considering what to say, but Melody had the strangest feeling that she was listening to some inner voice that might not be her own.

"Okay, you can leave it for now. I can't exactly afford to go out and buy my own stuff at the moment, so those secondhand things you scavenged will at least make the place look like someone lives there while I'm showing the apartment to potential renters.

"Melody, are you absolutely sure about this? This doesn't seem like anything you would *ever* do, and to say it's insane is an understatement."

Melody knew there was no turning back. She fought to avoid picturing what she had seen about Casey while linked with Michael. She envisioned the ocean with waves washing on the shore and the sun setting. That stilled her thoughts.

"I'm sure," she said. "When you know, you know. And Michael is…exactly the person I've been looking for." This was true on so many levels.

"Okay. But if you come back in six weeks telling me some sob story, I won't be surprised, and I *will* have rented your room by then. So you won't have anything to fall back on."

"Yeah, I know. I just don't think it's going to be an issue."

Melody was glad when the break ended and they returned to work. The rest of her shift went by without further conversation, and she got back on the road to Michael's just after 11:30. Despite next to no sleep the night before, he had waited up for her to arrive.

* * *

"Yes, I see the time streams," said Archangel Michael. "Too many of them still hold shadows. Would that it could be prevented."

"They have been warned at least," Metatron replied. "And we have dispensation to act when the opportunity is right. We could not ask for more from the Creator than we were given. I sing the praise eternal to the one light forever expanding."

"And I live the song of gratitude for the pure flame of the heart," intoned Michael. "For now, we stand with these children of light as long as we may and give all energy to their rising above what may come to pass if they choose unwisely."

"And so we shall guard them, my brother," Metatron replied. "And we shall love them enough that perhaps—even with that many time streams converging in the same manner—they may find their way."

"And so we love," Michael toned.

"And so we live," Metatron sounded.

"Always in light," they spoke as one.

Chapter Four

A Shadow Falls

Melody slept that night as though she were made of stone. She didn't hear Michael leave but had some sense that he had looked in on her before going out. She awakened just after 10, stirring slowly as was often the case when she managed to get nine hours of sleep.

Michael had left a note to let her know he had stocked up on food and that she could eat whatever she found appealing. After a quick breakfast, she grabbed her art supplies and went outside to catch the light. On her day off, there was nothing she desired or truly needed more than to draw in the sunshine.

She found an area with a few palm trees and a patch of lawn at the other end of the building and sat down with her pastels and drawing pad to work on the latest image that still sang in her brain like distant music that evoked feelings of pure love and joy. She dove into the stillness of the empty page, and soon the now familiar shapes began to form in an array of rainbow colors. Here in her world of art, she existed beyond time, it seemed, and everything outside herself—the noise of nearby cars, the distant roar of a plane overhead, even the feel of sunlight on her skin—gave way to the inner realm where her spirit toned the endless echo of creation.

As if awakened from some perfect reverie, she felt this reality tugging her back as a shadow loomed over her, claiming the light that bathed her drawing pad in its essence. She looked up to see a man standing between her and the sun.

"Sorry to interrupt," he said. "I couldn't help noticing you over here and wondered what you were drawing with such apparent focus." The stranger, who wore a friendly, pleasant smile, looked harmless enough, but Melody felt a shudder travel down her spine.

"I have a rule about showing my work before it's finished," she replied. "We artists can't bear criticism in the middle of a piece, you see. It would make us much less likely to complete the work."

She said this truth with a smile but hoped it sounded like a casual, lighthearted comment as well. She had the distinct feeling that this man was not meant to see her art—ever.

"Oh, come on. What if I promise not to comment?"

"Nice try, but I can always tell when someone likes my work and when they don't. Besides, I never break that rule." She smiled again although she felt like running and didn't know why.

The man appeared to be considering her statement. She had an overwhelming sense of needing to get away.

She looked down at her cell phone. "Wow, look at the time," she said genuinely surprised by the lapsed hours. "I need to be getting back to the apartment so I can be there when my friend arrives home. I had no idea I'd been at this for so long. I guess I should thank you for the interruption."

"All right then. Another time. If you change your mind, my apartment is just over there. Third floor, apartment K." He pointed to the building opposite Michael's.

"Well, that's not likely, but thanks for your interest—and for jogging me back to awareness about the time."

She closed her drawing pad and got up from the spot where she had been working, said "goodbye," and made her way as quickly yet nonchalantly as possible back to Michael's place.

When she got inside, a sense of relief washed over her. She wondered why on earth she had such a strong reaction to the man. She had not given him her name nor asked his, and thankfully he hadn't had a chance to offer it. But it didn't matter. She knew somehow without doubt that she needed to be away from this man and hoped to avoid him in future.

Opening her pad again, she went back to drawing. She skipped lunch as was often the case when she worked at her passion and completed the piece by the time Michael arrived home.

* * *

"Wow," Michael said when she showed him the image. "I've seen this," he said. "I've been there." He gazed intently at the page that was filled with such wonders. It looked as if it must be the realm where worlds were born. "So much light," he said. "I don't know how you create so much light. It's brilliant."

"Thanks," she replied. "I've been there too. As for the work, it isn't mine really. I'm only the hands that bring it onto the paper or canvas."

"Ah, but what hands," Michael said. "I feel almost like... like miracles could happen from just looking at this art. I can't tell you how much I love your work."

She was grateful for his words. But the gnawing feeling of a shadow passing into her day lingered.

"What's wrong?" Michael asked. "Are you all right? I got a really strange vibe just then like something was wrong."

"It's probably nothing," she said, but, even as the words came out of her mouth, she knew that wasn't true. "I was working most of the day outside in the sunlight, just sitting on the ground by those few trees near the building, and then some guy came up and started talking to me, and I just had this weird sense that I needed to get away from him and that I couldn't let him see the piece. I realize it must sound nuts."

"No, it doesn't," Michael said. He had an inner knowing that she was right.

"Listen, can you…*show* me?" He took her hands in his, palm to palm, and started to still his mind and quiet his feelings. Letting go of his day at work, of everything outside this moment, he sank into his heart and invited her to join him. Before long, they were breathing together and linking again as they had done on the beach with the tone of the hum filtering out the background noise of their minds. As she recalled the meeting, he was there with her as if looking through her eyes and experiencing her perceptions.

He became aware that Archangel Michael was sheltering her during the entire exchange, letting her know that she needed to be wary and reveal nothing to this person. He realized a blue light encompassed her as she talked with the stranger and recognized that the archangel had been directing her responses.

She inwardly spoke, "Thank you, Michael, archangel of protection. Thank you."

A thought, a knowing from Archangel Michael then reverberated within both their minds: "This man represents a primal, physical danger to you, daughter of light. Had you not been in my keeping, his nature might have revealed itself in ways I wish not to describe. You must learn to be on guard now, precious one. Retain your innocence; yet be aware and cautious."

Michael felt the contact begin to subside as did the sound of the hum he now associated with the archangels. Gradually he returned to his normal state and looked directly into the eyes that so mirrored his own.

A tear fell down her cheek. "I didn't think," she said. "I mean, I've always just sort of walked through the world without considering such things. Now I guess that will have to change."

He reached out and pulled her gently into his arms. He felt so close to her and understood exactly what she was feeling. He recalled having that view of the world a long time ago, but he had faced too many harsh realities to retain that sense.

"I'm sorry," he said. He wanted with all his being to shelter her just as surely as the great archangel had done earlier in the day.

"Thank you, Michael," Melody said. "You're a lot like your namesake, I think."

She seemed more at ease and like her light, airy true self again. But he still felt as if she had lost something. That sense of pure trust and pervasive innocence that so perfectly emanated from her just yesterday appeared to have departed.

"It's all right. I'm still who I am," she whispered. "Maybe I'm just a little less naïve than I was a day ago. I'll get over the change. It's really okay. It's not as if I haven't experienced my share of troubles." She took his hand in hers and smiled.

"For right now, though, I'm famished. It just hit me. I haven't eaten since breakfast and think I'd better remedy that pretty soon or my stomach will rebel with some serious noise."

"Well, I had lunch but I'm hungry anyway," he said. "How about we order pizza so we can have more time to talk and make plans?"

"Sounds perfect to me. And the sooner, the better."

Over slices of vegetarian pizza, the two shared stories of childhood and their more recent history. They decided that eating wasn't really conducive to anything more serious than that. He talked about his two younger brothers and their antics growing up. He was always the serious one while the two of them, especially Tom, the youngest, was more of a prankster who managed to get them all into hot water more times than he cared to relate. She shared tales of her younger sister and their favorite pastimes of playing make believe and dress-up.

"You won't believe this, but I went five years in a row as an angel for Halloween. That was always my favorite costume. I'm pretty sure those tattered wings are still somewhere in the attic at my parents' house in Boulder City."

"Actually, I don't have any trouble believing that at all," he said with a grin. "How could you have been anything else? As for me, I usually went as one superhero after another. But there was the year that I *had* to be a knight complete with sword and armor. Plastic ones, of course. My brothers and I loved to play with those. I guess we both had some sense of connection to our true selves even then.

"Where's Boulder City, by the way?" he asked.

"Southern Nevada. It's just 35 minutes from Las Vegas, but we rarely went there. Boulder City was a no-gambling town, and that suited my father just fine."

At the mention of her father, Michael sensed some gloom pass over her heart then swiftly depart as though she willed it away. He wanted to ask her about what he was feeling, but he had no desire to call that pain back into her bright heart.

Instead, he told her about growing up in Eureka in northern California, where he came to love his time in nature. He still found the greatest peace when hiking in the hills or walking by the ocean and wished he could live as close to the Pacific as she did in Venice Beach.

"Of course, that will have to change now," she said looking a little sad for this reminder.

"Sorry," he said. "I know my little apartment can't compare. I hope you can find a place that will. But…not too soon," he added. "I'd like to keep you around a little longer if it's all the same to you."

He realized he said that with more intensity than he meant to. But truth be told the idea of her not being close troubled him. He wanted more than anything to just have her by his side all the time.

"I feel the same way," she said quietly. "I've never been so at home in the company of anyone. I wish…"

"What if we got a larger place together?" The words spilled out as if he had no way of curbing his inner truth. Of course, she clearly could read his thoughts anyway. "My lease comes up for renewal in three months. I know it's not ideal having to stay here all that time, but I'm willing if you are."

"I would love to get a place with you," she said being every bit as honest and open as he was. "But I can't put you out for that long." A frown pinched her brow as she looked toward the bedroom and back at the couch.

"I really don't mind, and besides I'm going this weekend to buy an air mattress or maybe even a sleeper sofa. I haven't quite decided yet. But we'll work it out if you're willing. I don't think it's a good idea for you to be on your own right now. Okay?"

He took her hand and laid it against his heart. "You know I mean it, right?"

"I know," she said, tears brimming in her blue eyes. "All right then. We'll make it work. I'll look for a server job near here for now, and whenever you're ready we'll start searching for a place where we can move when the lease is up. I feel like the angels are guiding this decision, and who am I to question that?"

"Exactly," he said. "And I'm 100 percent sure you're right about them directing us. I feel like we're going to be able to find a place that's perfect too. Just one thing though. As long as we're here, don't go sitting outside unless I'm with you. Okay?"

"That's one decision I've already made myself. I'll find another spot to draw where I can feel more secure."

* * *

"The time streams remain unwavering," said the mind of Metatron. "The convergence of almost all possibilities still brings the same eventuality."

"Yes, I had hoped that today's intervention might bring a different result," Archangel Michael replied.

"If she loses faith, then so does he. There is no other potential among their futures," Metatron whispered into the heart of Michael.

"I will do all in my power to protect her, my brother."

"I know, dear flame of the Creator's heart. And I will imprint upon her mind all that is good and glorious for as long as her heart is open."

"There is yet hope," Michael said. "And where faith, hope, and love abide, light flows."

Archangel Michael expanded his wings of blue flame to their world-encompassing width. He felt all the children of earth in his massive heart. Every sorrow, every trouble, each cry to the Creator flooded his being as he held them all for just a moment, and in that instant all willing souls who suffered in pain felt loved.

"If only I could give them more," he intoned.

"I am the prayer for their deliverance," Metatron hummed into the universal core.

"And so it is," said Metatron and Michael as one.

* * *

True to his word, that weekend Michael went in search of a sofa bed while Melody was at work at the restaurant. As he hunted through a huge warehouse of furniture, he sensed his connection to her emotions even across the distance between them and had a strong inner knowing of exactly which couch she would find appealing. He smiled as he realized how similar their tastes must be. They shared so many traits and feelings about the world that it wasn't really surprising.

As he paid for the purchase, Michael noticed the sales clerk who helped him had shadowy energy around him. He did his best to ignore the sensation of being in proximity to something that seemed to fill the atmosphere around the man with a pervasive feeling of gloom. A strange thought came into his mind: *lost souls*. He tried not to dwell on it and simply paid for the furniture and delivery and left as quickly as possible.

This sort of thing was happening more often to Michael now. He'd always had an inner sense about people and an awareness about who could be trusted. But this was far more intense and obvious than anything he had experienced before the hum. And the most difficult part was that he was subjected to this sort of sensation wherever he went these days. Meeting Melody and connecting so powerfully to her seemed to have enhanced this ability with a much more acute perception.

Just after Michael got into his car to drive back to the apartment, he experienced the most powerful sensation. Suddenly he was somehow in two places at once. He was himself sitting in the car, and yet he was also in a restaurant smelling food emanating from the plates he was carrying on a tray that felt heavy, hearing snippets of conversation as he passed by tables, and sensing the energies of people all around him.

"What the..." he said out loud. And the act of speaking thankfully brought him back into his own reality. He was here in the parking lot of the furniture warehouse. He was himself. He was Michael. He touched his legs and pinched himself to be sure he wasn't dreaming.

"What was that?" he asked again out loud. As clear as if it were spoken, he heard within his mind, "Awakening angels can bi-locate. You and Melody became one for a few moments. Be unconcerned."

He knew the voice belonged to Archangel Michael. "Be *unconcerned*?" he said. "What if I had been driving?"

"Soon this will become easier. For now, know that it will only occur when you are not in a situation that would cause issue."

Michael experienced an overwhelming sense of security overtake him—as if his whole being were sheltered in an embrace so profoundly peaceful and reassuring that nothing in the world could disturb or diminish it. He breathed in that feeling and allowed himself to contemplate this strange new gift.

He smiled at the memory of all those years dressing up as comic book superheroes. All of them had unusual abilities that took them down a path of helping others. He supposed in some way this was what he had always wanted. It must have been ingrained into his soul, but how different it seemed from some fantasy on film or in the world of Marvel.

Feeling it was safe now to drive home, he made his way back to the apartment to await Melody's return. A sense of harmony that clearly was a residual effect of his visit from Archangel Michael lingered in his psyche, and he wanted to retain it for as long as he could, so he sat on the couch that had become his bed of late and decided to keep breathing the energy of his experience.

Within moments, he was back in contact with Melody, seeing through her eyes, experiencing her surroundings, when something unexpected happened. She started to inhale more rapidly, and a sense of panic rose in her chest as she looked across the restaurant. It took a moment for him to acclimate to her view, but he quickly understood the disturbance in her internal circuitry. At a table by the window seated in what he *knew* was part of her station, the man who lived in the building across the way was looking over the edge of a menu directly at her. She swiftly pulled her gaze away from him and down to the wait station where she was putting lemon slices on a small plate to take to someone's table. Anyone viewing from outside would think that all was normal, but Michael felt her emotions, her heart racing, and his own did the same. An urgent need to *do* something overcame him and drew him back from his connection with her.

Michael grabbed his keys and left immediately. It would take 45 minutes at least to get to her. He got in his car, found the shortest route via GPS, and hit the road. Trying to still his thoughts, he reminded himself that this was a restaurant filled with people, that she was watched over by angels, that nothing was really wrong. But he *felt* the wrongness. He couldn't shake it. Why was this man eating at a place so far away? How would he know where she worked? Michael's thoughts raced until a sheltering presence began to still his inner turmoil.

He said to Archangel Michael, "Why are you here with me? Please, go be with her. Watch over *her*."

"I am," said the archangel with a resounding sense of clarity. "If you are able to be in more than one place, do you doubt that I can? I am everywhere someone needs me—*always*."

"I love her," Michael said internally, knowing the archangel heard his every thought. "It doesn't matter that we just met a few days ago. I love her and would give my life for her."

"I *know*, my friend," the great archangel intoned in a stillness and quiet that nonetheless rang through Michael's being as though he stood next to a massive cathedral bell that was chiming intensely.

* * *

Melody sought to still her inner turbulence and regain her calm. It was too strange to be coincidence, she thought. Foreboding filled her mind and every sense seemed magnified. She could show nothing of her unease on the outside. She understood this.

Today she'd had the strangest moments when it seemed she was not alone—as if her new friend, who was so much more to her already, was *one* with her. It was an indescribable sensation. Even though this just happened for the second time, it was not uppermost in her agitated inner being at present. Inwardly, she was calling out for Archangels Michael and Metatron and seeking some way to both protect herself and understand what to do. She contemplated not waiting on the man, getting one of her friends to take the table instead. Although the idea was hugely appealing, she felt it would give away something and that she'd better just face the man herself. So she took the lemon slices to table four and immediately made her way to greet this man whom she would rather have never seen again.

Approaching him with what she hoped seemed like ease, she said, "Good evening. I'm Melody and I'll be your server tonight. Would you like to know our specials?"

"Why, I must not have made much of an impression when we first met," said the man. "Don't you remember me?"

"Oh, wait a second. Now that you're speaking, you sound familiar. I think we met on the day I was sketching. Sorry if I didn't recognize you. I was looking up at you with the sun behind you, and it was hard to get a good look at your face." She imagined this sounded plausible.

"Oh, well, I'm glad you recognized my voice at least," he replied.

"What are you doing so far from home?" It was a natural question, and she thought it might seem odd if she didn't make the observation.

"I was just in the area," he responded. "And, yes, I would like to hear those specials."

He grinned in a self-satisfied way while Melody went down the list as slowly and efficiently as possible. Somehow reciting the dinner specials seemed to occupy enough of her awareness that she could appear natural in the process, or so she hoped.

"I'll have the ahi tuna, but make sure it's really only lightly seared. I like a little life left in it," he said, again with a grin.

"I'll get your order right in," she said turning to leave as quickly as possible.

She felt a hand on her wrist clenched ever so faintly. "No rush," he said. "I'm not in a hurry. I have all the time in the world."

She turned only slightly and smiled as cordially as she could. Although every part of her wanted to shudder and usually she had great difficulty not revealing her emotions, she simply acted as casual as possible.

"The manager doesn't really like us to dawdle," she replied. "I'll be back with your salad in a few."

As she walked away, she felt his eyes on her, but she wasn't sure he was really the only one behind them. She fought the urge to let a tingle run up her spine.

Her shift ended at 9 that night, and he had come in at 8. Melody would have time to wait on him before getting off. There was no escape from the task at hand, so she simply went about the business of her job with complete focus.

She was pleasant each time she returned to his table. She had a strong feeling that she was getting unseen help to lighten her mood and demeanor when deep within there was an intense awareness of shadowy energy emanating from this man. Before connecting to Michael on the beach that night, she had never noticed such things. She saw only light in the world wherever she looked and was always able to tune in to that divine spark within the people she met. But she found none in this man, and that worried her.

Melody usually returned to check on customers several times, but she limited her visits to his table to the required amount. As she was preparing his check, she gazed up suddenly toward the entry door to the restaurant and immediately a rush of security passed over her entire being as in walked Michael Browne. Their eyes locked in knowing, and without so much as a nod she realized he understood everything.

Melody slid the bill for her unwelcome customer into its black leather sleeve and felt *real* ease this time as she walked to his table. For a change, this visitor wasn't looking at her. He had been watching her rather blatantly from the time he arrived, but now his eyes seemed riveted on the waiting area where Michael sat.

"I hope you enjoyed your meal," Melody said drawing his attention. "I can take this whenever you're ready," she added as she lay the tab on the table next to him.

"Hold on and I'll give that to you right now," he said. He paid in cash and added, "No change."

"Thank you," she said. "Have a good evening." She strolled away as nonchalantly as possible.

The clock by the register showed it was almost 9, so she asked her friend Denise if she would cover her last few minutes. Her manager was fine with her leaving a little early since things had gotten quieter. Melody was free to grab her things and go to Michael.

When she reached his side, he embraced her tightly. "I was so worried," he said.

"It *was* you, wasn't it? You were seeing through my eyes." She spoke softly into his ear so that no one else could hear.

"Yes," he said as he pulled away slightly. With almost a whisper, he added, "And I promise I wasn't trying—at least not the first time. It just happened spontaneously.... But let's not talk about this now. Could we just go home?"

"Absolutely!"

They had to drive the lengthy distance in separate cars, but Melody didn't feel alone. She could sense his energy from the vehicle ahead of hers, and the link they shared was almost tangible. As she drove behind him, she *felt* so much. The moment he had walked into the restaurant, she experienced such relief—but more than that. She knew she was falling in love with him. Truth be told, that must have happened the instant they met or perhaps at the moment they connected so deeply on the beach that same night. She realized she would give her life for this man if the need arose. She would do everything in her power to protect him as surely as he would her.

When they arrived home, the two of them noticed that the lights were already on in apartment K of the building across the way. Once inside, Melody felt she could let down her guard and relax, but she sensed Michael's state was still one of vigilance.

"Something doesn't feel right," he said quietly. "I feel like...I don't know. I just get the strong impression that someone's watching us."

He turned down the overhead light, which was on a dimmer, until it emitted only the faintest glow. Then, he walked across the room and peeked through the closed wooden blinds, lifting only a single slat the tiniest bit. The shiver that had threatened to rush up her spine at the restaurant finally got its way, and she went to the window to stand by Michael.

"I can't see anything. Can you?" she asked.

"No, but he's there. I sense him. He's not at the window with the light behind it. That would be too obvious. He's at the other one."

"Michael, what can we do?"

He allowed the slat to fall back into place and turned to her, taking her in his arms. And she let go of everything outside the moment and the feeling of his warmth and comfort, his securing embrace.

"Let's call our friends," he said.

What he meant was obvious. Keeping the light low, they sat on the couch and faced each other. His breathing quickly matched her own and both inhaled deeply and exhaled completely. His hands reached out for hers, and it seemed that both their palms and their hearts joined together at the same moment. She began to see light dancing behind her closed eyelids. First, a white glow beamed through her brain, and then it was joined by a brilliant blue illumination. Soon these energies could not be contained. They expanded through every particle of her body and his and then radiated through the space around them.

The energy was moving from the inside out and the outside in. Her heart/mind/spirit and Michael's were merging with the light of two massive archangels who now stood over and surrounded them. Both peace and electricity filled her. An ecstatic sense of being more fully alive than at any point in her human existence flooded her thoughts and feelings.

Metatron's voice hummed through her cells. "Still your feelings, my kindred, and open only to the love of divine reality."

She breathed more fully the light and the love that encompassed her. Then she began to look through her closed eyelids. She "saw" Michael sitting there facing her, yet he appeared to be composed of trillions of tiny particles that resembled stars as if every atom that formed his body were alive with its own brilliant, blazing blue-white sun. She turned her gaze downward to view her hands, which shone with the same radiance in pure white with sparkling rainbow colors shimmering from them.

"This is how we see you," Metatron resounded into her being. "Beautiful as ever."

Then, Archangel Michael's presence drew her awareness. His energy felt entirely different and yet somehow exactly the same as Metatron's. Both expressed the eternal song of love divine but each in his distinctive way.

Melody sensed Michael, her companion, looking at her just as she was truly, profoundly seeing him. Their connection grew stronger as she focused on it. But her awareness of the archangels still remained uppermost in her consciousness.

Then, Archangel Michael's words reverberated as a tone through their minds, hearts, bodies, beings.

"For as long as you abide in this place, it shall become your sanctum. I shall place my own protective fire in its very walls so that you can speak and live freely when you are held inside this lodging."

At that moment, blue flame shot outward from the space around them and filled the walls, floor, and ceiling of the apartment. A sphere of blue-white light expanded to encompass the space as well followed by an octahedron in the same color and then a double tetrahedron of pure white energy. All of these then disappeared completely.

The two archangels spoke as one into both Melody and Michael: "They have been made invisible so as not to draw the attention of anyone or anything that might wish you ill. We invite you to give intention and loving light each day to these defenses in order to strengthen these securing boundaries. We will always energize your efforts."

Melody and Michael embraced an infinite sense of love that blanketed their beings. And, then, the two great archangels departed.

Even after she sensed their exit, the residue of love lingered in her heart and in the space around them. Still linked with Michael, she knew that he experienced much the same.

They were slow to return to a normal state—not that anything could truly be called *normal* again. The visual images and vivid brightness behind her closed lids slowly dissipated, and both her own breathing and Michael's resumed its usual rhythm. Opening her eyes, Melody gazed at Michael and was able to perceive a soft white glow around him.

"How beautiful you are," she said.

He smiled. "Not the typical compliment I get," he said. "But I was going to say the same thing to you. You should have seen yourself a few minutes ago though. As lovely as you are with my eyes open, I've never even imagined what I saw when I looked at you through…I don't know. Was I seeing through my spirit or through Archangel Michael? I'm not sure. But either way—"

"I know. Indescribable is the word."

"And that's how they see us," Michael said. "It's hard to believe. So much life. So much light."

"I guess we really are made of stardust," Melody whispered. "Maybe someday I'll get to paint a portrait of us looking as we did just now."

For a long while, they didn't speak. Peering into each other's eyes and hearts instead, they lived in a place where language seemed superfluous.

"You know what we have to do, right?" Michael finally asked.

"Yes, reignite the protection every day together. I saw it clearly."

"Archangel Michael was sending signals into my consciousness through our connection, and I know that we need to be extra careful going forward. That neighbor *recognized* you. He followed you and waited hours before coming in to have dinner."

Melody suddenly felt queasy. She had wanted to believe it was coincidence, but she knew it really couldn't be.

"What do you mean he 'recognized' me?"

"He knows what you are or at least that you are *different* somehow. He recognizes you as, well, *light*."

"But then why wouldn't he recognize *you*?"

"He does," Michael said. His face appeared unconcerned, but Melody read his thoughts as if he were screaming them at her.

"Michael, don't worry. I'll be okay. I'll take whatever precautions are necessary. I promise."

She sensed him working to allow the concerns to dissolve. He kept reminding himself that she was protected by Archangel Michael.

"You know far too much about what I think," Michael said with a grin. "It's okay. I'm not going to spend all my time trying to protect you. Only as much of it as I can."

He laughed at himself just a bit, but it was enough to break the tension and let the energy of apprehension leave his thoughts.

"That's better," she said. "We know what we have to do, and we'll get through this. Count on it," she added.

She heard his thought as clearly as if it were spoken: "If only we knew how."

Chapter Five

Sunrise

Michael slept fitfully that night. It wasn't that he didn't believe in the help of the archangels. Accepting their assistance was a given—at least to his conscious mind. But his subconscious apparently found all of these strange occurrences disconcerting and overwhelming. Dreams of warring forces, light and shadow, tormented his sleep. He awakened at dawn feeling drugged with the need for more rest, but he found it unlikely that slumber would return.

As he lay on the couch watching the sunrise faintly washing the room more and more in its soft morning hues, he heard stirring in the bedroom. Soon Melody, dressed in a terrycloth robe over her gown, came to the bedroom door.

"What's wrong?" she said.

"What do you mean?" he replied.

"Michael," she said with a patient smile, "I can't sleep if you're worrying. Apparently, my consciousness has become so linked to yours that I may even be sharing your dreams."

He sat up and said simply, “I’m sorry.”

He couldn’t help noticing how graceful her movements were as she crossed the room and found a spot beside him on the couch. She reached out her hand and placed it over his heart.

“I’m not sorry,” she said. “I would rather have this gift than any other I can imagine. To be able to know what you are feeling, well, I’m thankful for it.”

Despite his morning breath, he wished he could kiss her at this moment. Instead, he put his hand over hers and smiled.

“It *is* a gift,” he said. But he knew she was already reading every word and emotion he wanted to speak just as he was sensing the love and peace she emanated into his mind. In the dimness, he thought he saw a single tear fall down her cheek. He experienced overwhelming gratitude expanding into his being. Whether it was hers or his own, at this point he couldn’t tell. All he could do was feel.

“Is this how our lives will be from now on?” he found himself asking.

“I think maybe so,” she replied. “I hope so anyway. I think somewhere deep inside I always knew this was possible even though I never experienced it until now.”

“I used to imagine something this profound, but I’m not sure I ever really believed it was possible,” he said. “I’m honestly still having a hard time wrapping my mind around it. But I suppose we’ll get used to it.”

In a hushed tone, he added, “I don’t think we should tell anyone.”

"You're right. Something tells me Archangel Michael may be whispering that into your ear."

He grinned at the thought but also recognized it could well be true. He didn't have the overwhelming sense of the vast presence of his favorite archangel, but he definitely had a persistent impression of being connected somehow.

"I feel that too," Melody said, once again clearly aligned with his perceptions. "It's like a part of me is here while another is somewhere out there with Metatron. I can't really put it into words, but I think it's the same with you and Archangel Michael. They never really leave us and we never really leave them."

They sat with this knowing for a while in the dimness, simply experiencing the peace of being in each other's company. Michael realized how fully Melody had integrated into his life in the span of less than a week. He was happier in these moments than at any time since drawing his first breath in this world—at least any that he remembered.

"Me too," she said quietly. She yawned. "Sorry, I'm still pretty sleepy. Do you think you might be able to go back to sleep for a while?"

Almost an hour had passed since they awakened, but this Sunday morning he might welcome some extra rest. The two of them had shared so many late nights and travels during sleep.

"Absolutely. I feel much more at peace now."

She hugged him gently and then returned to bed, and he quickly found himself dozing off after a handful of minutes. As he drifted into the space between waking and slumber, he heard the familiar sound of the hum, and let the message it conveyed permeate his inner being.

"I am ever guiding you, my friend. Hold your truths close between you, for on this path lies wisdom. Know that I am watchful when you cannot be and I see into every eventuality. Trust that I am with you," said the hum, and a blue as deep as the evening sky ushered Michael back into sleep.

It was more than two hours later when he awakened to the smell of coffee. Melody was dressed and looking in the refrigerator for something.

"I must have been dead to the world not to have heard you," he said. "I never sleep that hard."

She turned around to face him, shutting the door to the fridge. "You obviously needed it. So did I."

As Michael gazed at Melody, he wondered if perhaps sleep still colored his vision. A soft glow surrounded her in white and rainbow hues.

"You're a vision," he said. "Literally. I wish you could look through my eyes right now."

She stood there breathing deeply and closing her eyes until he felt her reaching out to him, merging somehow into his perceptions as if she had always been there.

"Wow," she said. "Now that's something." Then, he sensed her draw back into herself, and she crossed the room to sit beside him.

"Was that like what you did with me yesterday? I was looking through your eyes at myself for a moment. What a strange sensation."

"It was something like that," he replied. "But it probably feels different when you are the one receiving the experience. I can tell you I didn't want you to leave. It seemed so *natural*."

"I was surprised at how easy it was," she said. "I just sort of wanted to connect with you, merge my mind and yours, and it happened. I think maybe because you had already paved the way yesterday. That was awesome!" A tiny giggle arose from her throat and with it a burst of bright yellow breathed into the air around her.

He smiled and looked into her eyes that so reflected his own. The two of them decided to spend the day trying out their new gifts. After breakfast, they took turns merging with one another's consciousness until they started to get a little tired. They spent time connecting thought alone or only emotion but found it easier to convey both at once. The deeper form of complete linking required getting used to, so they decided it was better to use this method only on rare occasions.

* * *

Over the weeks that followed, they practiced daily communication with each other and with the archangels and shared a world that few could imagine. They devoted at least an hour each day to amplifying and reaffirming the protections Archangel Michael had built and to strengthening their spiritual bond with each other.

Melody found a job at an upscale restaurant nearby where she made good tips, and the two of them searched for a new apartment every weekend until just the right spot opened. The timing for their move was only a few days before Michael's lease ended, and everything seemed to fall into place. Michael was certain that larger forces were at work making it all appear effortless on the surface.

After the one incident in the restaurant, the soon-to-be former neighbor never showed himself, yet Michael had a sense at times that they were being watched and that he and especially Melody needed to remain vigilant. For her part, she chose different routes to her new workplace and usually waited on him to be available for shopping and other excursions. Even though almost three months had passed and she believed such precautions weren't necessary, he insisted on her taking extra safety measures, and so far she had continued to heed his advice.

Not long after they got truly settled in the new apartment, which was a little farther from his work but slightly closer to the ocean they both loved so much, the time came to finalize their plans for the trip to England. The typical weather for early December in the UK was cold and often rainy, and neither looked forward to the conditions on Glastonbury Tor, which would be a drastic change from the climate of Southern California. Nonetheless, from a more profound perspective, their anticipation of the journey grew daily. Archangel Michael still had not told them what to expect or why they were going. Michael sometimes wondered if archangels liked to surprise people. In any case, he supposed they would have to learn what awaited them as it unfolded.

Michael's workdays passed slowly and tediously. Every moment away from Melody or filled with the concerns of the mundane world seemed wasted to him now. He decided to make a habit of connecting to Melody on his lunch break every day. To save money for the trip, he generally took a sandwich or a microwavable meal with him to the office, so it was easy enough to go out to his car both to eat and shift his energy in order to reach out to her across the miles. She generally worked later in the day and could be at home and ready to open to the union of thought and feeling at the appointed time.

Today, however, she wasn't there when he stretched his mind and heart to link with her. She was off entirely that day, so her absence seemed more than odd. When he expanded his inward search and still couldn't locate her, he started to feel worried. A thousand "what ifs" rose in his mind, and, being the protector and worrier that he was, many of the scenarios he imagined were less than joyful. He knew such thoughts would do her no good under any circumstances, so he did his best to quiet them.

His breath became slow and even, deep and full. He forced his heart and mind to open only to divine light, and he sent out the call to the one who always answered, reaching upward toward the heavens and joining finally with the archangel he knew so well.

As soon as he felt the fullness of light that is Michael, the archangel, he asked, "Where is she? Why can't I find her?"

Quickly he was wrapped in a blanket of serenity and security, an overwhelming sense of peace flooding his consciousness.

"All is well, my friend," said Archangel Michael.

Michael's consciousness was then directed to Melody's location. She was in an art gallery. He perceived every room in the space all at once and then homed in on Melody herself, portfolio in hand, sharing her work with what was clearly the director or curator of the gallery. An immense sigh of energy and breath released from his chest when he saw her there obviously safe and unharmed.

When he connected as lightly as possible with Melody, she became aware of his concerns and inwardly reassured him and explained what had happened. He understood that she had received a call and was invited on the spur of the moment to come to this place. It was an opportunity she couldn't pass up. He sent feelings of encouragement and love to her and then gently released the link.

"I'm sorry to call you for nothing," Michael inwardly spoke to the archangel.

"To calm your inner turmoil is indeed to call me for *something*, old friend. You know I am ever here for you, yet I must remind you that turbulence in thought and emotion only feeds that which is in shadow. It is wise to call upon me *before* what you would call 'jumping to conclusions,'" Michael intoned into his being.

Both of them smiled, a smile that came from knowing one another beyond all boundaries and being of one mind in the sharing of a truth.

"I'll do my best to remember that from now on," Michael said. "Of course, it means undoing more than two and a half decades of human thinking. But I guess I can do it."

"You were made for the task, after all," said Archangel Michael, still smiling into his namesake's heart. "I recognize it is a challenge to be both vigilant and aware while at the same time free from concern, yet you are more capable than most humans in this regard."

For several minutes, Michael enjoyed the companionship and energy of his forever friend and teacher. As they communed, he always learned, or rather remembered, the truths his soul already knew. Each time they communicated, their bond, which was established so long ago that Michael's conscious mind could not fathom such a span, deepened and became more a part of his human existence.

As a result of his lengthy contact with his mentor, Michael had to gulp his lunch in order to get back into the office on time, but a little indigestion was definitely worth the exchange with the magnificent archangelic presence. After work that day, he was anxious to see Melody and hear about her meeting, and she was equally eager to share her experience.

"The gallery director came across one of my angelic paintings at a friend's house, she said, and she wanted to see more. When I showed her my photos of the work and some of my sketches, she got super excited and actually offered to host a show for me! I could hardly believe it."

"I'm so happy for you, Mel," he said.

"She had an unexpected opening in her schedule around lunchtime, so I jumped at the chance to go in and meet with her."

Melody paused. A look of concern etched her lovely features.

"I haven't signed a contract or anything yet though. I…I wasn't sure. You see, I had a strange feeling while I was there. And, no, I'm pretty sure you know I don't mean when you connected to me. That was awesome. I didn't get a clear signal on my cell when I tried to call you, so I was glad you checked in.

"It's just that when I shook her hand, well, I don't know how to put it really. I felt a coldness wash over me. I mean, everything was fine the rest of the time, and it was only for a moment, but I thought it could mean something. So I put off the idea of doing anything contractual even though I *really* want to have a show there. I'd rather wait until you meet her and see what you sense."

"Can you recall your feeling clearly?"

"Sure. I rarely feel anything like that, so I think it is etched pretty firmly on my memory."

"All right, then; let's connect and let me get the impression you had."

Michael sat opposite Melody and joined hands with her. They began their usual process, breathing in unison and reaching for each other with heart and mind. It was so like something out of *Star Trek* that he had commented on it several times. *Shades of Deanna Troi*, he thought. Behind closed eyelids, he sensed Melody inwardly smiling at that fleeting notion.

As she went back to the gallery in her mind, he walked with her into the director's office, saw the woman's face clearly and dove into the feeling that accompanied the shaking of her hand. He sensed immediately what Melody meant. It was like shaking the hand of a robot, or at least he imagined it so. No warmth. No genuine feeling. The smile on the woman's face was broad, but there was nothing behind it, nothing to lend a sense of true emotion. Just emptiness.

Michael drew back from the moment and slowly exited Melody's memory. He opened his eyes to look at his favorite face in all the world.

"That's *different*," he said. "It was like a vacuum, a void. I can sense evil, but I don't know what to make of this. I don't think that kind of absence of emotion can be a good thing. But I honestly don't know what to make of it."

"Exactly," Melody said. "She said all the right things, you know—everything an artist could want to hear about her work. She made the idea of a show there sound really appealing, which it would have been anyway. But the whole time I kept feeling like something was missing or *off* somehow, and I couldn't figure out just what. She actually told me that an artist had backed out on a show last minute, and she has an opening for a show to begin the first Friday in December, which, of course, would coincide with our trip. I knew I couldn't tell her about that, but I did say that that was probably far too soon for me to put a show together. I could do it, but…"

"Yes, but with a capital B," he replied. "It seems somehow a little too *convenient* for an opening to happen at that exact time."

"I know. But how could anyone know about our trip and what it's about when we aren't even sure of the purpose behind it? Still, it crossed my mind too. If some dark force wanted to stop us from making that trip, what better way to entice me to stay here? I think maybe I'm getting paranoid. It seems a little crazy, doesn't it?" she said.

"Not to me," he replied. "But, then, I work for the protector archangel, so I tend to err on the side of caution as you know." He smiled to lighten the mood.

"Maybe we should ask," he added. "Who knows if they'll tell us or ask us to 'discern for yourselves' as they so often do, but it's worth asking, I think."

This time they went into the deepest meditation they could manage. Michael had taken some psychology in college and remembered it was called theta state. The brainwaves slowed to that level near sleep but they were still conscious. Over the course of the last few months, as they worked together and with the archangels, Michael and Melody gradually had gained the ability to move quickly into that space of serenity, where they could more easily connect to the angelic realm. Each time the high-pitched hum greeted their shifting of consciousness and ushered them into a reality outside their normal awareness.

Michael felt himself lifted up. He knew he was still in his body, but the physical aspect of his being seemed far away from his current vantage point. He found himself in that place beyond time, the space of stillness, the eternal now. Melody stood beside him, her form glittering with pastel sparkles in pure white light. Before them, the two leaders of the archangels, Michael and Metatron, their teachers and friends, towered over them. Archangel Michael's wings of blue-white flame extended into what seemed infinity. Metatron's immense pillar of white light stretched surely beyond the boundaries of the universe, or so it seemed to Michael's human perceptions. And somewhere so far beyond the reaches of his faculties to discern, a pure white sun shone this brilliant stream of light into existence.

All around them, light streams passed through this ethereal place in every color of the rainbow. Shimmering pathways, glowing corridors in both brilliant and soft hues, moved through this seeming junction between worlds.

"Yes, a very astute perception," Archangel Michael intoned.

Metatron added, "We are indeed at what you might call the hub of the wheel of life and the universal gateway. What you perceive are the radiations of divine light that travel through all existence in order to paint your world and the whole of this universe in those frequencies that invite *divine* reality. The glowing orbs you see passing among the seas of energy and riding their waves are angels and other beings of light on their missions to assist humanity and all life. We wanted you both to remember this place, for you are always a part of it."

Michael felt Melody's joy expanding as he stood beside her. She emitted waves of radiant bliss that permeated his being. He knew she belonged here. He looked into her glistening eyes of cobalt rimmed blue and saw the perfection of her being. In those eyes, he could perceive worlds and galaxies without end. And all of it flawless. Love filled his heart as though it might burst into pure flame.

He realized he needed to pull his gaze from her, that there was, after all, a reason for their being here beyond this ecstasy of the moment. It was difficult, but he did so.

"You know why we came," Michael said to the archangels. "We need to understand. Is there something else we have to be aware of in the world?"

Archangel Michael's heart of divine fire expanded a stream of pure blue flame to Michael and Melody's hearts and minds, and the sound of the accompanying tone held a unique frequency that happened when the great protector was sharing about these kinds of things.

"We cannot tell you *all*, dear ones, yet we can share this: There are two distinct types of issues facing your world. One you already understand. It is that which breeds chaos and perpetuates and amplifies fear in its many forms. These you have encountered. But there is the other, and it is more difficult to discern. These are the ones with but one task: to rob humanity of *humanity*, to take away all feeling of true love, hope, joy, compassion, and kindness. There was a time when the former was our main concern. Now the latter is equally prevalent and much more dangerous, for it is all too easily hidden, and it allows human beings to fall prey to their baser instincts and blocks their finer emotions. If taken to its extreme, the person who submits to this kind of shadow becomes a shell, a vacuum without any real emotion."

Although as a human Michael processed this knowledge in words, these truths were conveyed instantly in the angelic way as a whole unit of understanding, encapsulated and received fully in the moment.

Archangels Metatron and Michael intoned in unison: "There is only one way to defeat both of these types of entities. Love. Love beyond love. It is what we are. What you are. You are the defenders of earth, beloved friends."

Michael and Melody looked at one another and back at the archangels. Together they said, "But surely *you* are the defenders of earth."

"And *we* are one with *you,*" the archangels spoke. "You are the emissaries, the intermediaries. You are members of our legions on earth."

More fully than at any point, Michael felt the burden of the task before them. He wanted so much to do exactly what he came to do—whatever that might be.

"It will unfold in time," said the Archangel Michael. "For now, we can advise you that it is possible to deal with those who are influenced or deeply attuned to the shadow, but it is necessary to be cautious and aware of every detail when you choose to interact with them. And remember to avoid *all* judgment. You cannot know why they chose such a path nor can you afford to judge any soul. You are meant to rise above this even in the world of form."

"I will do my best," Michael said.

"And so will I," Melody added.

"We can ask no more of you, beloved friends," Archangels Michael and Metatron intoned.

"Let nothing dissuade you from your path or your plans. *Nothing,*" Michael, the archangel, added.

"Understood," said Michael.

With that final word, Michael felt himself being drawn back down. As swiftly as he had risen, he returned to his body even more quickly, and Melody and he gradually came back into a more wakeful state.

"I know I say this every time, but *wow*," Melody uttered softly.

Michael couldn't find words, but he knew their link remained strong enough that he didn't really need them. The hum still vibrated inside his brain.

Melody squeezed his hand. "You need to come back," she insisted. "You're still too *out there*. Let's go outside. I think you need to put your feet on the ground."

He felt a little unsteady when he got up but soon was able to regain his equilibrium. Much like the old apartment, there was a patch of ground with a few trees outside their new place, so they went to that spot and sat on the ground for a few minutes. Michael took off his shoes and felt the grass and earth beneath him. It definitely helped.

"Better?" asked Melody.

"Absolutely. I guess I didn't want to come back—at least not entirely. The more we go back to where we came from, the less I really want to be here, you know."

"Oh, I know only too well," she said. "But we have to be. They need us to be." She gazed upward in the direction of the sky.

"Yeah. I was born for this. And I'll do my duty. I couldn't really do anything else. But sometimes, well, it definitely feels better there than here."

Melody didn't answer him. She just put her head on his shoulder and snuggled closer. It was the perfect thing to do, of course, because it reminded him that here was not such a bad place to be—with her beside him.

"If you don't go anywhere, I promise not to either," he whispered.

"I'm right here," she replied. "The only travel plans I have are being bound for England in the dreariest time of year to go." She laughed softly into his shoulder.

"So what will you tell the gallery owner now that we know a little more about what's going on with her?"

"Cutting right to the point as usual," she said as she sat up. "Well, I will tell her that I'm honored she wants to feature my work and that I'd love to do a show in the new year but that I simply have too much on my plate to get one ready in time for December. I think that sounds pretty reasonable. Right?"

"I know it must be super hard to say 'no.' Hopefully, it will work out for later. If her intentions are not just to keep you from going on this trip, then I imagine it will. And we'll be extra careful in dealing with her in any case."

"Definitely."

* * *

The next few weeks went by at a speed approaching that of Metatron's whirlwind of white light. Melody was able to find people to cover all her shifts at the restaurant during their trip and had no trouble getting out of the gallery show.

The woman who directed the space seemed disappointed but polite about her decision. She wasn't altogether encouraging about when another opening for a featured artist might happen, but Melody was learning to trust the universe to take care of such things. If she was meant to have her work at the gallery, it would happen when she could participate. As much as she wanted her art to find a larger audience, she was concerned about having it represented by someone who clearly was not aligned with the light.

At last, the week of their departure came, and Melody's stomach was obviously a breeding farm for butterflies. She sensed that Michael felt much the same, a heady mixture of anticipation, jitters, and angelic presence constantly looming. His way of dealing with things was to make lists and check things off one by one as each task put them closer to being ready. Her process was to dive into her art at every opportunity since it allowed her to focus and let go of everything else in those moments when anticipation overwhelmed her.

Her final items to pack were her small sketchbook, pencils, and pastels. She couldn't go anywhere without those crucial objects since she had no idea when Archangel Metatron might send her another image to recreate. Her sleep reverberated with tonal energies and accompanying visuals from those divine visits.

Just before she awakened on the morning of their flight, Melody dreamed of flying above the clouds. It was clear and bright and felt familiar as though she had soared beneath the sun countless times. She awakened feeling reassured and certain the journey would be smooth and secure.

"I love those flying dreams," Michael said. "And I agree. I suspect our plane will be the most protected vehicle on the planet."

His eyes were smiling at her, which always ushered a profound sense of joy into her heart.

The traffic on the way to LAX was thick, but somehow they found things flowing more easily than on most days in Southern California. The terminal buzzed with life amid the comings and goings of people from all over the world. The air around Melody and Michael felt electric, and their blended auras, together with the familiar over-lighting presence of the archangels, cushioned the very atmosphere, securing them in a way that was difficult to describe. Melody was reminded of the saying, "Be in the world, not of it." Those words seemed to fit best.

Melody normally had difficulty navigating spaces filled with people, so she focused on what was directly in front of her and saw that the path was outlined in a soft white light that appeared only to her. And to Michael, she suspected, but, under these conditions, she dared not link to his consciousness to check.

Instead, she decided to simply tune in more acutely to what she could sense within herself as she moved through the massive airport. The more deeply she went into her heart and mind, the more she was able to discern around her. She started to see trails of energy in every direction possible, lines of light crisscrossing one another in a way not unlike those light streams she and Michael observed at the hub of the universal gateway. But here the colors seemed less vibrant and true and were mixed with smoky hues that dulled and shaded them. Dark streaks also moved among the lighter colors, blocking the view in certain areas. She knew what these represented and didn't want to gaze into the shadows, so she drew her awareness back to the mundane as she and Michael proceeded to the gate.

After a long period of waiting, as they prepared at last to board the jet, she detected an unmistakable glow of electric blue and luminous white all around it. As Michael had said, their plane was likely the most protected vehicle on the planet.

Flying in a machine hardly compared to the soaring she experienced in her dream the previous night. She gazed out the window at gray-tinged clouds and recalled the freedom she felt when she was lifted high above the earth into a state far beyond this one. Sitting beside Michael, his hand in hers, she imagined them soaring together and sensed that he was picking up on her thoughts. She wanted to make their link stronger, but she heard his voice in her mind saying, "Not here. We are being watched."

She didn't open her eyes because she knew she would be tempted to look around and search out the reason for his statement. Instead, she simply breathed the stale air of the plane a little more deeply and wished the journey could be shorter.

After 15 hours and one stop, they finally landed in Bristol and caught a bus to Glastonbury. After they arrived, they found the day cooler than they had imagined, and a frigid dampness seemed to settle into every part of Melody's thin frame. It had been a long while since she had left the gentler climate of Southern California. Michael shivered right along with her as they tried to huddle as closely as possible both for heat and connection.

"Not my kind of weather," Michael said. "That's one of the main reasons I left Northern California and moved to L.A. Lucky I still have my cool weather gear."

Although Melody's body was having difficulty adjusting to the drastic change in conditions, her spirit felt a warmth emanating from this place. She sensed Michael did as well.

Luggage in tow, they made their way to the bed and breakfast just a few minutes' walk from the town. They had chosen the perfect place. It was called Tordown. Glastonbury Tor itself rose steeply behind it with St. Michael's Tower perched upon its summit. It felt like the archangel himself was standing watch over the place, and Melody could sense his presence here with them just as surely as Michael did.

The welcoming appearance and energy of this small inn and healing center greeted them with its homey embrace. Thankful beyond words to enter the heated Victorian house, the two of them knew instantly this was the right choice. Among the décor and surroundings were statues and pictures of angels and crystals that radiated a soft, clear energy.

The innkeeper smiled genuinely as she welcomed them. "I'm sorry to say you just missed the Frost Fayre. It's the last Saturday in November. I hope you two weren't hoping to attend."

"No," Michael said. "We're just here to see the sights."

"Well, there's plenty to see here any time of year," said the woman who introduced herself as Cheryl.

"We're putting you two in the malachite room since you requested separate beds. It's a bit pricier, mind you, but it has a lovely view over the Vale of Avalon. I'm sure you'll be happy with that one.

"By the by, you and my husband share the same name: Michael. I suppose it's sort of ideal for us living so close to St. Michael's Tower. He's around here somewhere and can help with your bags if you'd like."

They politely declined the assistance, expressed their gratitude, and made their way up to the top floor and into the quaint, cheery bedroom decorated in soft yellows, sages, and deep malachite greens.

Melody and Michael had looked at the pricing and descriptions for the accommodations and knew this was the likeliest space for their needs despite its higher cost. They were maxing credit cards to make this trip, but she had a sense of security about it and felt certain the funds would be replenished somehow.

"Alone at last," Michael said as they entered the room and surveyed their surroundings. "But, of course, never really alone," he added in a lower tone.

They had made plans regarding their arrival before leaving L.A. Melody rolled her bag out of the way and sat down on the nearest bed as Michael did the same. He faced her, his eyes a perfect copy of her own. The room felt warm, and quiet overtook their senses as they began to breathe together.

"I've missed this all day," she whispered and then closed her eyes.

Within moments, the link between them, the familiar sense of oneness that had become so much a part of their lives, deepened. They breathed as if a single person existed rather than two. Their hearts, minds, spirits merged and expanded into the space, moving outside of time, where they found, as always, the archangels who called them kindred and welcomed them with complete knowing of their innermost essence.

Michael, the archangel, intoned the unspoken language at once so familiar yet still foreign to the human aspect of being. It was music to the heart within them.

"It is time to secure the space. You know what to do."

Although the energy of this warm and loving place was as clear and beautiful as they had ever encountered, Michael and Melody knew shields were essential so long as there was shadow in the outside world. Just as they did at home every day, the two joined with their archangelic companions to establish a protection around themselves and the room. By now, this had become second nature and happened with ease. All boundaries around them—walls, ceiling, floor, windows—held them in a kind of safety zone in which they could speak and commune freely with each other and their companions.

Then, Metatron appeared in the foreground of Melody's awareness, imprinting a visual reminiscent of a glowing snowflake contained inside a star tetrahedron of golden-white light floating on a sea of cobalt blue.

"Carry this image within your heart and mind while you are here, for its impression shall be etched upon this sacred place as a homing beacon for those who seek to live the light. It shall call to them to come here and imbibe the elixir of life that emanates from the wellspring eternal. You carry the song of this forever in your own heart, child of light, and your presence here is as important as your companion's."

All too quickly this profound connection to the archangels eased and faded, and Melody found herself, still joined with Michael, back in a semi-conscious state in their room at the inn. She opened her eyes and looked at him. He often went even more deeply into the connection than she did, so his lids were slow to raise.

Ever so gently, she removed her hands from his and brushed her palm lightly against his cheek.

"Come back, my love," she whispered. "We need to ground ourselves now."

His eyes opened and his gaze poured all his being into her. That's what it always seemed like when he looked so intently into her eyes, especially at such times as these after the still wondrous engagement with the archangels.

"Don't worry. I'm back. *Sort of* anyway. I guess between the long trip and this different kind of journey I may be a little wiped out. I think I could sleep for a week."

In that moment, the weariness of the journey seemed to overtake her as well. "So could I. I don't think I'm up to unpacking or even brushing my teeth."

Then, she realized they were supposed to sleep now. This was part of the program so to speak. There was energy that could be processed only while they were in that deepest state of rest.

"Yes," said Michael as he shared her thoughts. "I get that too."

Without so much as changing into their night clothes, they both went to their twin beds and fell into the deep abyss of nothingness.

Chapter Six

Glastonbury

Michael was momentarily disoriented when he awakened after 12 hours. The unfamiliar surroundings did little to help him until he gazed to his left and saw her there asleep on the bed next to him. Then, the trip and everything else came into clarity. Through still heavy lids, he watched her breathe. Letting his eyes go out of focus, he perceived the aura around her, a field of soft white filled with pastel shimmers so like a bubble blown by a child's toy. The look on her face was one of such innocence. *Pure of heart*, he thought. *How did I get so lucky?*

She began to stir after a few moments and appeared almost as perplexed by the environment as he had been, but then she turned toward him and her eyes sparkled as clearly as always.

"Could you be any more beautiful?" he asked as he reached his hand out to her. The twin beds were side by side and almost touching, so it was an easy stretch.

She clasped his hand and smiled. "I suspect I look pretty much a mess after that sleep. But, fyi, you are beautiful to me too.

"I'm starving. How about you?" she added.

"Do you really need to ask?"

"Then, let's see what we can do about getting something to eat."

After showers and a quick change, the two headed down to the front desk to inquire about where to find breakfast. This time they encountered the husband manning the check-in area.

"Well, you're quite late for breakfast, but we saved some for you anyway. After a long flight, our guests often sleep in the next day, and we like to hold breakfast for them. Let me show you to the dining room."

The proprietor led them to a table that was already set for them.

"I'll just let Cheryl know to bring your breakfast as soon as it's reheated a bit. We've got some lovely vegetarian fare for you as requested. If you'll excuse me, after that I need to get back to the desk as we have a few other guests coming in today."

The woman whom they met upon arrival soon brought steaming oatmeal, orange juice, tea, and a selection of muffins to the table. Michael and Melody devoured the food as if they hadn't eaten in ages, which was how it seemed to him.

It was two days before the appointed time to visit St. Michael's Tower, and the plan for now was to walk to some of the other local attractions. Despite the damp and cold December, Michael felt an inner warmth churning as he and Melody made their way along the shop-lined streets of Glastonbury. They browsed a bookstore that looked like something out of the Harry Potter novels, another place with gems and jewelry that emanated radiant energy and calmed the senses, and a shop filled with angel art. Melody was particularly delighted with this spot. Her eyes sparkled with excitement as she perused the shelves and walls covered with figures that felt like home.

While she was browsing, Michael went to the cashier and asked about speaking with the manager.

"You found her," said the gray-haired woman with bright blue eyes. "I actually own and manage this place."

Michael pulled out his phone and opened the gallery filled with photos he had taken of Melody's art. He glanced around to be sure she wasn't within earshot or view and started to scroll through the pieces one by one as the owner looked on.

"These are remarkable," she said. "Are you the artist? I've never seen anything so…luminous."

"Actually, my girlfriend is the artist. She's over near the back of the store absorbing the wonders that line your walls and shelves."

"Does she have prints available of her work? I'd be interested in selling them if she does. These are truly extraordinary."

Michael felt Melody's energy moving closer to him and turned around to see her smiling with a glimmer of "I caught you" in her eyes.

“Could you possibly be talking about me?” she said looking at him with a sly grin.

“Yes, I should have known you would catch me. I was just showing your work to the owner.”

“And I love it, by the way. I’m Dorothy Stone. I have to say your art speaks to me, and that’s not something I say lightly. Do you have prints I could sell? This is a rather rash decision for me, but I’m drawn to your work and believe others will be as well.”

“I have made prints of a few of them and can do the same with others once we get back home to California. I’d love to have my work available here.”

Michael watched as Melody’s warmth and enthusiasm, her very essence, interacted with the shop owner. The two quickly made arrangements and exchanged information that would lead to having her work available on the other side of the Atlantic. He sensed the strong connection they were making and knew instinctively that this was a mutually beneficial arrangement.

By the time they left the shop, the two of them felt buoyed by the experience, and their inner lights danced down the street together as they strolled arm in arm to their next stop, a small vegetarian café called Rainbow’s End.

After a bite to eat, they made their way to Glastonbury Abbey, which was just a few blocks away. As they walked among the ruins of the ancient monastery, a hush descended on them. Amid the stillness of the place, they could sense all the lives of those who had passed long ago, the tones of their voices united in song. It was as if the monks still dwelled among these remnants of the great abbey that was. Michael felt such a reverence for this place.

Melody paused and leaned against one of the stone walls. "I'm sorry," she said. "It's just so much. I *feel* them. Their energy is so enmeshed with this place."

"I know. I sense it too," he replied. "I feel their final days and their last breaths on this earth. But I feel their *lives* too."

"Yes. It's the same for me," she said. "I'm all right now," she added. "I just needed a second to collect myself."

As they moved on through the ruins, they visited the burial place of King Arthur, or so legend has it. And they believed it was true, for they sensed a great spirit of light had touched the site.

"You know, I loved the tales of King Arthur and his knights a lot."

"That's not a big surprise," Melody said. "He certainly seems a likely character to resonate with Archangel Michael. The sword Excalibur definitely seems to carry that energy of the sword of light."

Michael imagined that mythic king coming to life, Excalibur by his side. He could perceive the vision with such ease.

"I see it too," Melody whispered. "As real as yesterday."

They stood in silence invoking a blessing for that long-gone king—whether real or merely an archetype built by the imagination of countless people who wanted to believe in something finer.

The clouded gray sky shifted into shades of orange, pink, and violet as the day began to wane, letting them know closing time for the abbey was approaching. They determined to return here before their stay ended.

On their way out of the ruins, Melody touched the walls by the entrance and imparted the vision she had seen with Metatron on the previous day. Michael could discern the image translating itself into the stone and moving down into the grounds below. Suddenly the whole abbey took on an ethereal glow and a golden white and blue field surrounded the entire place. Although Michael knew this was invisible to the naked eye, it was as clear in his mind as if it were a part of their tangible reality.

"So that's what Metatron meant," Melody whispered.

"I'd definitely say that's a 'beacon,'" Michael said knowing his words were an understatement.

As they left the abbey grounds, they realized this place would live in their hearts as it once had for so many who passed through its doors.

Before returning to the inn, the two of them discovered a spot for a light meal to carry them through until the next day. As Rainbow's End had been lunch, 100 Monkeys also seemed as if it had been designed with them in mind. It was a bit noisier, however, and Michael found himself wanting to return to the quiet of their room to seek the solitude they shared alone together.

Once they arrived back at the bed and breakfast, they saw another visitor checking in. His accent sounded like it might be Spanish or perhaps Italian. Michael wasn't sure. When the man turned around, he smiled genuinely at them and revealed something unexpected. His eyes were an incredibly vivid blue rimmed in a deeper shade of cobalt, and he looked like he could have been Michael's slightly younger brother.

Melody gasped almost imperceptibly.

"Buonasera. Good evening," the man said. "My name is Michel DeRosa. It is a pleasure to meet you."

"Michael Browne. And this is Melody Childress. We're happy to meet you too."

"I can't help noticing that you two look like you could be brothers," Melody said with a grin.

"Yes, you are quite right. It is remarkable, I think," replied Michel. "And we even share a name, it seems."

Michael felt an instant kinship with the man in front of him. He knew there was something interesting going on at a higher level here but said nothing about that. Instead, he and Melody said they hoped to see Michel the next day and made their departure to the room they shared.

"Okay, well, that was interesting," he said as soon as the door closed behind them.

Her smile reminded him of a childlike Madonna. It embodied qualities of serenity and enthusiasm, inner knowing and naiveté at the same time. His heart warmed automatically when he looked at that smile.

"Something definitely is going on," she said. "Isn't it exciting?"

"Yes. I just wish I understood more. Archangel Michael doesn't seem exactly forthcoming when it comes to satisfying my curiosity though."

“I’m feeling like we just need to wait and see. I know there is a reason for us being here right now, and it will be revealed soon. We just have another day to get through, after all, and, although I’m definitely as curious as you, I have this strong sense that waiting is best now.”

“I know,” Michael replied. “I realized it before I said anything. But it doesn’t stop me wanting to know what is happening. I guess that’s just how my mind works.”

He loved the way she looked at him. Always understanding. Sometimes his heart flamed with so much heat and love that he felt he might explode. The expression on her face, the same feelings expanding into him with every gaze, told him everything he needed to hear without a single word.

Despite the lengthy sleep the night before, they retired early again. Michael sensed their day would begin as the sun rose, and they needed to be fully present. Their hands touched across the inch or so between their beds, and he felt reassured by that gentle contact, the simple human touch that evoked so much more beyond the mortal world. *Someday*, he thought. *Time outside of time and always one.* Those were his final thoughts before drifting off.

* * *

“The gathering is at hand,” intoned the Archangel Michael.

“One by one, all will hear and heed the call,” said Metatron in the language of light.

“But are they ready?”

"You know the answer as well as I," Metatron replied.

"Possibilities upon possibilities upon possibilities. Free will is both glorious and terrible. I have no wish to live as they do," said Archangel Michael.

"Nor do I, my brother, yet while they are embodied, it is all they know of existence."

"And where has it brought them? To the precipice. Again," Michael intoned.

Archangel Metatron expanded his airy white light to fan the fires of the heart of his kin, the keeper of the blue flame of the Father. The two linked fire and light, heart and mind, to a harmonic of complete Creator essence.

"This time we will succeed. We will surely avoid the darkest time of shadow and death. The earth shall know peace. The 144,000 shall arise and complete the mission." Metatron saw the wavering light streams and infinite potentials just as Michael did, but his divine mind could accept only the eventuality of success—no matter the odds.

"By Creator's will, so shall it be," Michael spoke.

"And so it is," they intoned in unison.

* * *

Melody awakened later than expected at 8:00 in the morning. She surveyed her surroundings, taking in the warm atmosphere this cozy space provided. The sun was just rising and their room wore a pale peach tint that colored the day in a shade of optimism. The sunshine yellow bedspreads added a bright touch against a backdrop of sage green wallpaper banded with a border of cherubs and dark, malachite-colored curtains and pillows. There was a kind of honeyed sweetness lingering here as though someone had taken great care to imbue this place with a feeling of warmth and kindness.

Michael was already up and in the bathroom shaving. The sound of him clearing his razor on the sink must have stirred her, or perhaps it was those gentle rays washing her eyelids into wakefulness. It was good to see the sun again.

She slipped into her robe and went to stand beside Michael, her face appearing next to his in the mirror.

"Good morning," she said. "I guess I still wasn't recovered from the journey. Either that or this place has a profound effect on my sleep. I didn't even dream, or if I did I don't recall it."

His eyes met hers in the reflection, and he smiled through shaving cream. "Same here. I could hardly believe it."

After getting ready to face the day, they went down to the dining room for breakfast. As they entered, Melody immediately noticed a flower of life design hanging on the far wall. Two sunny windows drenched the peach-colored room in tones of gentle, welcoming radiance.

Michel from the evening before sat at a table beside the farthest window, and two other new faces were situated nearby. One man had a bronze complexion and long, straight brown-black hair. Melody thought his eyes were particularly distinct. She would swear even from a distance they seemed to have glints of amber among the deep umber.

At the table next to his, a beautiful woman, who appeared to be around Melody's age, sat by herself. Her hair was almost the same length and texture as that of the man she hadn't met. Oddly, she too seemed to have eyes that gleamed with some inner fire. Melody thought perhaps this was just her imagination. She smiled at the woman as she and Michael walked by to find a table.

"Won't you join me," invited Michel. "Please. I know no one here, and you are about my age, I think. I'd love to have some company."

Melody truly would have preferred to sit alone with Michael, and she sensed he felt the same, but there was no reason to deny such a polite request, so they found themselves sharing breakfast and making light, pleasant conversation with this stranger whom they had met the previous evening. Somehow it felt like the right thing to do in any case.

It turned out Michel was from Northern Italy. He worked in his family's business and still lived with his relatives including four sisters and one brother. He said he had come to Glastonbury for a holiday although there was something about the way he worded this that implied more than was spoken.

"Yes, we're here to see the sights too," Michael said. "We visited the shops in town yesterday and walked through the historic abbey. Today we hope to make an outing to the Chalice Well and its gardens. It looks like a better day for it than yesterday was. At least the sun is out."

"Isn't it strange that we chose December for such a holiday," Michel said. He looked as if he wanted to inquire about something more but remained silent.

"Well, I suppose it's a good time of year to avoid most of the tourists and to get off-season rates," Melody interjected with a smile. She had learned that telling some truth often satisfied people when the full story could not be shared.

"Yes, very true," Michel replied.

Throughout the meal, as unobtrusively as possible, Melody eyed the other two visitors, who had kept quietly to themselves during breakfast. She felt drawn to them. Although she knew it was best to stick to the mundane aspects of life when outside their room, she couldn't help slowing her breathing and going within to a degree to see what she might discern. As she deepened her awareness, she had the definite impression that Michael was doing exactly the same thing. *Like minds*, she thought.

She sensed a luminous energy around both of the other strangers and around Michel. But there was something else. She couldn't quite distinguish what it was. She kept hearing in her mind the words, "silken strands connecting all." But she was quickly drawn back into the conversation and lost the thread of her thoughts.

As the meal drew to a close, Michael said, "Well, it's been a delightful breakfast, Michel. I hope you'll excuse us now. We want to get an early start on sightseeing."

"Of course. Buona giornata. In my language, that means have a good day. I hope to see you later." Michel stood as they rose from the table and then returned to his seat to finish his coffee.

They bundled up with scarves, gloves, and winter coats. Even though the day was mild for this time of the year by Glastonbury standards, the air felt crisp and frosty to two people used to Los Angeles weather. Melody was thankful that Michael emanated that inner fire that so often warmed her cold hands as well as her heart.

They walked briskly along the route toward the Chalice Well, which was situated 10 minutes from the inn. A chill wind swept through the street as they made their way.

"I'm not sure what's happening, but I know something is. I often wish the archangels would clue us in more about things."

"I agree," she replied. "I guess it's on a need-to-know basis and we don't need to know," she added with a giggle, thinking back on having heard that in a lot of spy and detective movies.

"One thing I can tell you though. It only just hit me. Since we got to Glastonbury, I haven't seen or sensed any of *them*," Michael said furtively. "Not a one. And to be honest, I've seen them *everywhere* lately. But so far in this town I have yet to sense a single person who is overtaken by the shadows. Sure, there were a few muddy-looking energies here and there yesterday as we went through places, but no one who was like your former roommate or the man who lived across from us at the old apartment complex or the gallery owner."

"That's pretty extraordinary in and of itself, isn't it?" Melody asked.

"I'd say it's downright amazing. If it weren't so frigid, I might actually want to move here."

He half smiled and she knew he meant it at least a little.

"I'll keep my eyes attuned to my inner awareness, of course, but I think we may have found, at least for right now, a kind of safe haven. I hope I'm right."

"So do I," she replied. "So do I."

They walked the rest of the way in silence. The grounds of the gardens surrounding the Chalice Well revealed a beauty that even the cold of this time of year could not diminish. They had viewed photos online that were taken in summer when the flowers blossomed around the well and grounds, but even this season without those showy blooms had its special magic.

The arrangement of the greenery and the stones, the patterns of interweaving foliage in circular formations—it all evoked a sense of home in Melody's heart. Everywhere the double interlocking circles, the insignia of the place, brought the feeling of unity and harmony. She and Michael held that perfect sense of knowing that these outer expressions represented the inner light they themselves shared in their moments of profound union.

There were hidden treasures around the grounds as well—a tiny waterfall, fountains and pools, and a meadow bench with the perfect view of the tor and its high tower. After walking for a long span, they even found a covered shelter with a bench where they could get at least partly out of the chilly breeze. They huddled together there, his arm reaching around her reassuringly.

"Someday maybe we can return in summer," she whispered through slightly chattering teeth.

"You were reading my mind again," he replied.

"No, not this time. Just thinking out loud. But I suppose it's hard not to pick up your thoughts too at this point," she replied. "This place really does feel like a sanctuary, you know. I have such a sense of belonging here."

"Yes, I feel much more grounded here. It's like…I don't know exactly. I guess my senses are somehow diving into the earth beneath us," he said, his voice a soft hush almost lost on the wind.

"I get that but there's more. It's like I can feel the water below us, and I am a part of it. It flows in my veins."

He leaned his head against hers, and her senses experienced everything—the strands of his hair caressing her forehead as the wind blew them, the warm pocket of air from his breath, the energy of his heart and spirit merged deeply with her own. No kiss could have embodied so much love as this moment held.

"I know," said Michael.

They sat there in the stillness and bliss of their connection to each other and the place.

"We need to actually go to the wellhead itself," she said at last. "It feels like the right time."

They meandered to the center of the gardens and through the wrought-iron archway leading to the Chalice Well. As they entered into the field of energy around it, they discerned a soft white light filling the entire area.

Hands and hearts joined together, they moved into its soothing luminescence and sensed the presence of a sacred energy.

They stood by the well opening—for how long? Melody knew she had risen outside of time into the perpetual peace that was her nature.

"I am here," the familiar ring of Metatron resonated through her mind, yet it was more than this. The eternal spirit of pure essence washed through her very being.

She looked into Michael's eyes and saw tears flowing slowly down his cheeks. She could feel the wetness on her own face too. As they stood there by the well, of its own accord the divine design given to her by Metatron formed around them with its three-dimensional snowflake inside a golden-white star tetrahedron and both within a sphere of brilliant electric blue. It moved through them and into the stone enclosure and the waters below, spanning out to encompass the place. And in this embrace, Melody found the greatest harmony she had ever known in this world.

The tears did not abate until the visualization, which was palpable to her senses, seemed to dissipate and disappear, yet she knew, they both knew, that it was simply becoming integrated into every particle of this sacred site.

She gazed down at last at the cover to the well, its exquisite design seeming to echo the union of their energies.

"The Vesica Piscis," Michael said. "Heaven and earth, spirit and matter made one. No wonder they show it everywhere around this place. It's such a perfect symbol for how I feel right now."

"And the sword or lance with a heart at the hilt," Melody remarked, "pays homage to the tower, I suppose. How I love it here."

They had seemed untouched by the wintry wind for a while as Metatron's image washed over their beings and surroundings, but soon the chill returned and seeped into them, and they realized it was time to find a warmer haven.

They had searched online in advance and found another vegetarian restaurant with organic foods nearby. The Excalibur Café offered vegan burgers fit for a Pendragon king. The soup replenished Melody with an inner warmth that extended all the way to her fingers and toes.

She watched Michael as he measured the space and recognized that he was sensing the energies around them even while they ate. A part of him was always watchful and aware as if on guard. *No doubt the angelic side of his nature, the protector at work*, she thought.

Before they left, they ordered a vegan pizza to nosh for dinner later. Then, they retired early to the Tordown for an afternoon rest and arrived just as yet another party close to their own age checked in. The couple appeared to be from South Asia. The woman wore a sari beneath her cloak. They turned to look at Melody and Michael as the door shut the cold outside behind them.

Melody couldn't help noticing their eyes. The same glints of gold shone amidst the deep brown. The woman's irises were in fact truly amber rimmed in a rich deep bronze. This made her appearance particularly striking.

Melody and Michael smiled and nodded to the new arrivals and then traipsed up the stairs to the top floor.

"Yes, I saw their eyes," Michael said as they closed the door to their room. "This is a little surreal. I'm getting the strongest impression that we're all here for the same thing."

"Me too," she said.

His own eyes were lit by an inner fire that was always there, the same kind of radiance that gleamed in the irises of the other visitors. She could hear his voice in her mind say, "And in yours, my love." She smiled at him as though the heart within her could somehow be conveyed through her expression.

"It is," he whispered. Or perhaps the words were voiced inside her head again. At times, when she peered into those eyes, all she could perceive was the true spirit that lay beyond them in such harmony with her own.

He put his arms around her and pulled her close to his chest, where that inner fire glowed ever so brilliantly, and her mind and being were washed in blue-white flame.

* * *

Michael's intention had been to lie down for a brief doze, but the last rays of the sun were retreating swiftly behind the tor by the time he managed to open his heavy lids. Thankfully, Melody had turned on a small lamp, so he could get his bearings and return more fully to a waking state. As he did, he reached out with his senses and couldn't find her. Then, after expanding his inner awareness just a bit, he sensed her below him somewhere on the first floor. He focused entirely on her, his feelings for her, his appreciation of the beauty and light that she was, and instantly he touched her consciousness with his own, the sensation of connection renewed.

He felt her reaching back to him and knew that all was well. Quickly collecting himself, he tromped down the stairs to find her. She sat on the plush sofa in the lounge, gazing into the fireplace as fingers of flame rose and receded, dancing to the song of crackling wood. She appeared rapt by the display of vivid golds and oranges with the occasional edge of blue.

Melody must be rubbing off on me, he thought. *I'm thinking more like an artist every day.*

At that moment, she turned to him and smiled, a knowing look radiating from those pure blue eyes. He crossed the room and sat beside her, and she leaned against him, returning her gaze to the fire. His nose detected the pleasing scent of peppermint in her hair from the shampoo she used.

"Your hair always reminds me of Christmas," he said.

"Well, I do love a candy cane," she replied.

Then, he too joined her in becoming transfixed by the blazing logs. They must have sat like this for half an hour without outer conversation. Inwardly, however, they shared their impressions—the joy of deep warmth rekindled in their bones, the wonder of just being together in their own inner world, the taste of heaven in the closeness they shared. A huge amethyst quartz heart rested nearby, and they could sense it amplifying their love and inner light into the space. It seemed deeply in tune with them.

Michael could have stayed there happily for hours if not for an interruption. They reacted simultaneously as the large entry door opened and frigid air swept into the space.

A woman with warm brown eyes and a radiant smile entered. Her clothes looked too light for this climate, and she appeared to be visibly shivering. Towing her suitcase behind her, she headed for the check-in desk, and quickly Cheryl emerged from nearby to welcome her.

“You must be Ms. Tsdhuma,” the proprietress said. “Come in and get yourself warm.”

“Please call me Anaishe,” the woman responded, her accent obvious although Michael wasn’t familiar with its origin. “I was not prepared for the cold wind. I’ll be fine now that I’m inside.”

“Well, I hope we can remedy that. You’ll be in our citrine room, and it’s well-heated. You’ll find a roaring fire in the lounge. It’s just through there. You may see my husband Michael pop in every so often to tend the fire.”

The woman gazed toward the fireplace and then at Michael and Melody. He felt her indecision as though she didn’t want to intrude.

“Please, come join us,” he said. “This weather can take some getting used to.”

“Yes, please do,” Melody added wearing her most welcoming smile.

"Thank you," the woman replied. "I would love to get warm. In my country, we do not have this kind of weather except at higher altitudes."

"Where are you from?" Melody asked.

"Zimbabwe. I run a travel business there that arranges tours mostly for Americans and Europeans who want to visit. In Harare, where I live, the temperature was almost 40 degrees higher when I left than it was when I landed. I am afraid my warmest coat is not sufficient here." A perfect, broad, and genuine smile brightened her face. "I will get used to it perhaps."

Melody said, "The weather in Southern California is significantly warmer than this too. We've been here two days and still haven't acclimated."

"Well, perhaps not, then. I will do my best."

"What brings you to Glastonbury this time of year?" Michael asked. He immediately regretted doing so since it could prompt Anaishe to wonder the same.

"Well, I have always wanted to come here."

Michael noticed that she didn't actually answer his question, but there was something more there hiding behind her eyes, which gleamed with an inner light. He knew it was time to change the subject.

"What does your name mean? It's beautiful," Melody said, obviously sensing his thoughts.

"My mother told me it meant 'who is with God.' I've always liked that. But she is the one with God now. She died last year about this time." Her voice trailed as tears welled in her eyes. "I am sorry. I cannot help missing her sometimes."

"Please forgive me for bringing up a sad reminder," Melody replied.

"Oh, no. To remember my mother is a good thing. She worked so hard and gave me so much. I am thankful for her every day even now that she is gone."

Melody reached across to the other sofa and put her hand over Anaishe's. "Thank you for telling us. If we can help you feel less alone while you're here, please let us know."

Anaishe appeared somewhat surprised by the gesture but nodded graciously. "Thank you," she said after a few moments. "That is very kind."

After that, there seemed no need for words, and they simply sat there welcoming the heat of the fire until Anaishe announced she would like to go to her room to unpack. They wished her a good night and decided to retreat to their own space as well.

The now tepid pizza was nonetheless a treat as they sat together in the malachite bedroom.

"I instantly loved Anaishe," Melody said between bites. "I felt so at home and at peace with her. She's got an unusual demeanor, I'd say—both highly energetic and serene at the same time."

"You mean, kind of like yours," Michael replied with a chuckle.

"Well, I suppose we do tend to enjoy people who are like us. But it was just so *comfortable* being around her. You know how with most strangers you feel you have to fill the conversation every second, and you don't always know how?

But I could just sit with her and say nothing at all. That's a rare quality, I think."

"You know I felt the same. Definitely something special about that one and not *just* the gleam in her eyes."

"She had that for sure though. Shining eyes with glimmers of light in them. It seems to be a thing around here."

After dinner, Michael felt strongly the call from the archangels pulling them into the peace that lived somewhere high above them and equally in their own hearts. He and Melody joined in harmony and settled swiftly into the routine of strengthening the protection for the space and for their own beings. Soon Michael sensed the rush of energy, the flaming heart, the endless presence of the eternal, and he rose into its light knowing that Melody was by his side.

The archangels always seemed vast beyond comprehension although they revealed themselves in a way the human aspects of Michael and Melody could understand. Their impossibly tall forms shone in luminous splendor, and Archangel Michael's wings of brilliant blue flame filled the atmosphere of this ethereal space.

"Beloved kindred," the great archangel spoke—though the sound was more an intonation translating itself into language within Michael's mind and heart. "The time of the beckoning is at hand when the 144,000 must heed the call in order to fulfill the mission. Tomorrow shall be a profound beginning."

Metatron continued, "We have welcomed you here into our midst once again because the two of you are essential aspects of this activity. You will learn more at the appointed moment. Arrive at the tower atop the tor no later than the hour of 12 in your human time. You will not be alone."

Michael felt his heart widening as it filled with more and more pure white light and vivid cobalt fire. *How can I hold all of this*, he wondered. *How could any human being?*

And the resonance of the Archangel Michael's words echoed into him, "My kinsman, you are not truly human. Yet, even if you were, you would be made of the same stuff as we, the very essence of creation's heart. You are simply accepting more of that which you already are."

As Michael brought his attention to Melody, she appeared to be dancing within a whirlwind of radiant white luminescence. He had never imagined anyone so beautiful or perfect. She too was becoming one with the energies that flooded her. A stream of opalescent energy poured directly into her head and coursed through her entire being, and she seemed to float on waters made of light.

Beloved, he thought. And her gaze shifted to include him. As it did, he became a part of her airy light stream and she a part of his expansive flame. Then, the archangels surrounded them both with their energies in unison, the air and the fire fueling them with such a conflagration of creation's mind and heart that Michael could scarcely withstand it. And, yet, somehow he did. Love beyond imagining resounded through his being as he and Melody were gently and slowly drawn back down into their bodies.

Always such encounters left him feeling stretched beyond physical limits, his body an electric grid of connected, endless currents. Every cell was alive with the feeling of motion, and he imagined it went all the way to the atomic level. Each time he found it more difficult to return from the ethers. But she was beside him. Her hand in his warm and tangible yet just as much a part of that current of energy as his own.

Michael wasn't certain how long it took him to open his eyes, but, when he did, hers were there looking back at him, the greatest joy and peace in them that he had ever seen.

"Beloved," he said aloud.

"Michael," she answered. "I'm here. Always here."

Her hand grasped his more firmly and he repeated the gesture of solid reassurance.

"Don't ever leave," he whispered.

"I promise you I have no plans to be anywhere other than at your side for whatever is to come."

He felt her heart reach out to him with a feeling that made words seem small.

"Heart to heart, mind to mind, soul to soul," she murmured.

For what must have been minutes or perhaps hours, they just lay there gazing into each other's eyes, complete in their unspoken communication and union. Two blended souls outside of time.

Finally, knowing they had to be rested for the day to come, they prepared for bed and drifted once again into the deepest of dreamless sleep.

Chapter Seven

The Gathering

As the rising sun stealthily stretched its rays into their room, Melody felt its light tiptoeing over her eyelids. She moved quietly out of bed and over to the window. Surprised by what she saw, her mouth opened in an almost soundless gasp, but that was enough to awaken Michael.

"Up already?" he asked, rolling over to face her.

"Yes, and I was greeted by sun and snow. I didn't see that coming," she added.

"But it was clear yesterday," Michael said as he raised himself and started out of bed to join her.

"I know, and it is again now as you can see, but the ground is covered in that unmistakable blanket of white."

"Well, at least it's stopped, and there isn't enough to keep us from our hike. Hopefully, some of it will have melted by then."

"I think it's supposed to be here—just like we are. The snow has a cleansing effect and also makes it far less likely for people to visit the tower today, I suspect."

"True," Michael said. "I doubt many people want to traipse up that major hill with snow on the ground. I'm glad I brought my hiking boots."

Melody smiled. "So am I. But I feel like it will be easier than we think. I hope I'm right," she added as she gazed at the covering of snow.

After coffee in their room, they went downstairs. That morning at breakfast, Melody and Michael made a point of seeking out the other strangers who were staying at the inn. Before leaving their room, they agreed it was likely these other visitors were here at the same time for a reason.

As luck—or perhaps angels—would have it, the other couple they had seen briefly were entering the dining room at the same moment as the two of them.

"Won't you join us for breakfast?" Michael invited with his most welcoming smile.

"That would be delightful," the man said, his wife nodding in agreement.

As soon as the four were seated, they introduced themselves. It turned out the couple was from Northern India. His name was Baiju and hers Aasmi.

"It's wonderful to meet you both," Melody said. "I hope you don't mind me saying this, Aasmi, but you have the most strikingly beautiful eyes."

The woman turned her gaze downward but smiled. "Thank you. It's very kind of you to say."

"My wife is always shy about compliments, but I tell her this all the time as well," Baiju said.

Melody sensed a deep affection between the two of them similar to the feelings she and Michael shared. While her imagination was known to work overtime, it seemed to her their brown and amber eyes shimmered even more brilliantly when the two of them looked at one another.

The conversation remained light throughout the meal, but Melody sensed a current of energy running beneath the surface and started to hear a hum that sounded both distant and fully present within her. Michael nodded to her as the ringing began, and she motioned the same in return.

"Do you hear that sound?" Aasmi asked her husband. "It's just like before only fainter."

He nodded to her. "I'm sorry. We don't mean to be mysterious. It's just...well, everyone remembers the 44 days of ringing ears. My wife and I actually became profoundly affected by it. We spent an hour or more each day in silent meditation allowing the hum to overtake our senses. It was powerful. But perhaps this seems strange to you."

"Just the opposite," Michael said. "We found each other because of that hum. It means a great deal to us."

Melody was about to share more when the strikingly beautiful young woman they had seen at breakfast the previous day walked into the dining area. She moved to a table near the wall several feet from them.

"Would you excuse me a moment, please? I'll be right back."

Melody walked the short distance to the woman and reached out with her heart, sending a feeling of calm warmth and inviting energy.

"Hi, I'm Melody. My friend Michael and I are visiting from the United States. We were hoping to get acquainted with everyone who is staying at the inn while we're here. Would you be willing to join us? I'm sure we could squeeze in another chair?"

"Thank you so much for asking me. I didn't want to intrude. I've been feeling awfully alone here without knowing anyone. My name is Tomiko. I came a long way too—from Tokyo."

The four of them made room at the table for one more, and Melody introduced their latest arrival. She and Michael exchanged meaningful glances again as they both noticed the hum increase its volume. She saw Tomiko put her hands briefly to her ears.

"You hear it too then?" Michael asked.

Tomiko's voice was hushed as she spoke. "Yes. I believe it is communication from the angels. When I dream of them, I always hear this sound. I believe…they were singing to the whole world a few months ago. I hope you don't think I'm crazy. That is just what I believe."

All five of them looked intently at each other then, and the hum grew louder.

The moment was interrupted when Cheryl entered with more food to put on the table. She smiled at the group and said, "Now this is what I like to see—our visitors getting to know each other over breakfast. It's times like this that make us glad we decided to open this place."

She was in and out quickly and conversation resumed.

"I have seen something about everyone who is staying here," Tomiko added. "Your eyes—every one of you—are remarkable."

"As are yours," Melody said. "We noticed too."

The sound of the outer door shutting was accompanied by a blast of cold air that managed to filter in even to the dining area. After only moments, the other man Melody and Michael had yet to meet walked to the entry of the room, surveying the place as if to discern where best to sit.

He headed at last directly towards their table. "Any chance you have room for one more? I think I'm supposed to join you."

Michael and Baiju said together, "We'll make room." They stood and pulled another table over to adjoin the current one, and everyone rearranged themselves a bit.

After the man introduced himself, Tomiko asked, "Where are you from, Yas?"

"Northwest New Mexico," Yas replied. He pulled a long leather strand out of his pocket and tied his long hair back away from his face.

Melody noticed again those deep brown eyes with flecks of amber.

"Where have you been this morning?" Michael asked.

"I love to walk in the snow. As soon as I saw the ground out my window, I went outside. It made me feel more at home here."

Cheryl obviously had heard the door as well and came in carrying another tray of breakfast goodies. She was gone as swiftly as she arrived and was smiling the whole time.

No one spoke for a while after that. Obviously hungry from the chilling walk, Yas appeared to prefer to eat in peace. It was during that silence that Michel and Anaishe arrived. Two tables of four were brought together allowing just enough space for all of them to find a spot.

Melody had pretty much finished her meal by the time Anaishe and Michel joined them. The hum, which had become less noticeable while everyone got settled, now resumed its louder, more obvious pitch. She knew exactly what she had to do. She began to breathe slowly and evenly as inwardly she called to her beloved Michael and to the archangels. Her thoughts and feelings immediately linked to his, and she could feel the presence of the great beings of light more fully. She had a sense they had been there all along, but the energy was enhanced by the more conscious connection.

"Yes, I agree," Michael said without using his voice.

"I hear you," Tomiko chimed in. Melody turned towards her new friend and smiled. Tomiko clearly had not spoken aloud either. Her eyes gleamed their inner light.

Anaishe stared at Melody. "What is happening?" she said aloud. "I am feeling waves of energy in my body. And my heart is so…open. Like I love you all without even knowing you. I cannot explain because I do not understand this. I feel like love is the only thing I am made of. I realize you do not know me and this sounds mad. Please forgive my unusual comments."

Aasmi, who ended up next to Anaishe after the table was rearranged, reached her hand out and touched Anaishe's arm gently.

"We all feel it, I think, perhaps in different ways, but I understand you completely." Melody nodded as did everyone else in the group.

"And the sound," Anaishe said. "It has come back even stronger than when the world could hear it. Do you hear that too? It speaks inside my heart."

Yas answered first. "We all hear it, I expect. I've been waiting for this. The elders talk to me. They always have. But this is stronger than their voices. Since the world sound happened, I have seen visions I can't explain. I go out under the stars and the universe seems to open to me."

Yas continued: "You all need to know something about me. I don't tell people my secrets. I keep to myself. I practice the old ways of my people, the Navajo, as much as I can, and we don't open ourselves to strangers. But… you aren't strangers to me. I recognized you when I first saw you, and I waited until the moment was right."

His eyes seemed to bore into the consciousness of each of them as his gaze passed every face in turn. There was a flow of energy moving around the table, through each one of them, as if an electric current connected them all.

"I recognize you too," Melody said in a hushed tone. "I didn't realize until Yas said it. I think I was supposed to forget until now. I've seen all of you before, but I don't know where."

"It was not in this world, I think," Baiju uttered softly.

The vibrational tone grew louder and shifted octaves. Tomiko put her hands to her ears. "That's a little loud, my friends," she said, and the resonance lessened slightly to a manageable pitch.

"Someone knows how to get our attention," Yas said. "I see the white eagle and the blue hawk soaring in my mind's eye."

Melody closed her eyes and caught a glimpse of the vision. "Metatron and Michael—the archangels," she said.

Michael added in a voice as low as possible, "Archangel Michael sent us here. What about each of you?"

Tomiko nodded. "I knew I was being guided by angels to come here, and it had to be now."

"It was the same for us," added Baiju.

"Years ago, when I was just a kid, the elders told me I would go to a far-off land in the time of cold and meet my kindred there. I started seeing visions during the world hum and knew the time was close. Then, one day I just knew when and where," Yas said.

Anaishe had tears brimming in her eyes. She said softly, "It was my mother who told me to come. At least it *felt* like her—so warm and kind and filled with love. That was how she always was. I dreamed of a pink light glowing so brightly and the gentlest spirit. When I awoke, I knew what I needed to do."

Melody and Michael listened as these brothers and sisters from afar told similar stories with unique twists and experiences. They inwardly communed with each other on a deep level and reached out with open heart, mind, and spirit to the others as they shared the road to this place at this exact moment.

The energy became so strong and focused around their table that every one of them felt it as a palpable reality, and all shared the vision of light around them—each in a different color of the spectrum. Melody thought it was the most beautiful thing she had seen on the earth—as vivid as the most magnificent sunset. She wished she could take a snapshot of the moment in living vibrant light to paint a portrait of the perfect essence that each of these souls shone so fully.

Tomiko said, "You are the artist. I knew one would be an artist. I felt it somehow."

Melody nodded. She longed to let go of words and dive more deeply into the moment, to live in the silent space between breaths and just hold on to this feeling of family, true family, forever. She felt Michael's hand squeeze hers gently.

"We need to prepare for our excursion up the tor," he said. "And I think Cheryl wants to clear our plates now." He looked toward the kitchen and saw the door barely ajar. Inwardly, he sent the message to all the others to join them on the walk up to St. Michael's Tower.

"We'll need to dress warmly," Melody said quietly but audibly. "Anaishe, you mentioned not being prepared for the cold. Do you have something you can wear? If not, I have some warmer things you can borrow."

"That would be most kind," Anaishe replied.

"What room are you in? I can bring some things to you."

"I am in the citrine room," Anaishe replied. "Thank you so much."

"We'll meet in the lounge in an hour to head up if that sounds good to everyone. The innkeeper told me it will take us about 30 to 45 minutes to hike up via the trail. I'm guessing closer to 45 given the snow."

They all agreed. It was difficult to end the link they had established and leave the table, but, even after doing so, Melody felt their energies still lingering with her as if they were still bonded albeit less intensely than when they were in close proximity to one another.

Back in their room, she and Michael simply gazed into each other's eyes and felt like home had found them here so far from the place they lived.

* * *

As they changed into their warmest clothes, Michael felt water running down his face. He hadn't realized he was crying. He felt elated, not sad. He wiped a tear from each cheek, but more took their place.

"Oh, my love," Melody whispered, her face covered in tears. "You're feeling with me. It's the joy, you see. It's almost too much. I can't retain it all in my mind and body."

He embraced her and held her close to him, letting the tears wash over him, and the feelings that were hers and his as one immersed them in an overwhelming bliss. Whatever came to them in the future, whatever strange turns they encountered on this journey, if they could hold on to this moment, they could weather it all with grace.

"It's almost time," he said at last, his arms still wrapped around her waist, his heart still linked to hers. "We should get ready."

After completing the last of their preparations, including taking warm clothes to Anaishe, they joined the rest of their party downstairs in the lounge and all headed outside into the bitter wind. The sun had disappeared from sight, and clouds again hovered above them.

Michael led the way with Melody beside him. Yas gained on them and soon walked in step with the two of them. The day hadn't warmed enough to melt the snow, so the trail was still covered but easy to follow. As all eight of them huddled close on the steep path, the hum started to vibrate through them. Michael noticed that it soon became like a chorus of tones as if the pitch resonated in a distinct frequency through each person in the group. The closer they got to the summit of the tor, the louder the hum became, and the warmer the energy that filled their beings and protected them from the elements. The snow began to fall again just as they reached the top and its flakes quickly grew in size. He wished for shelter but soon realized his heart light could reach to his extremities and serve as a blanket.

As he caught sight of the entrance to St. Michael's Tower, he saw four figures already standing there. For a moment, he felt concerned, a fleeting sense of alarm passing through him. But immediately the flame in his heart expanded, and he knew all was well.

Coming closer, he noticed instantly that one of them had eyes like his own while the other three had that familiar glint shining from theirs as well. One stranger's irises were emerald, and the other two were soft brown with golden specks. Soon all of them gathered inside the ancient stone fortification.

The tower walls stretched high toward the sky, but something quite odd happened when Michael and the others looked up. The open tower had no snow falling into it, and the sun appeared to be shining directly overhead.

"Excuse me a second," Michael said. He walked back out of the tower. From the outside, he could see no sun—only the snow drifting down in large flakes. Returning to the inner area of the tower, the sun radiated overhead, and there were no snowflakes in sight. The space was warm as if heated by immortal fires.

Tomiko said, "That is one miraculous and happy thing. I wouldn't believe it unless I experienced it. It feels about 20 degrees warmer in here."

The four new faces gazed with anticipation at the group. The green-eyed woman with dark auburn hair approached Melody.

"Have we met before?" she asked in what sounded like an Australian accent. "You all seem so familiar—especially you."

Melody responded with her usual friendly warmth of spirit. "Yes, well, I think perhaps we have, just not on this plane of existence. I don't mean to sound so strange, but that's the truth as I see it."

"Ace! That's a really good answer. I like it. And it seems about right to me. There are plenty of strange goings-on these days in my life, I can tell you.... By the way, the name's Grace."

"I'm Melody, and this is Michael."

Introductions began including the other three newer faces. A Brazilian man named Samuel Santos, whose aura shone in an aqua light, Sophia Rodriquez from Argentina, who glowed in soft peach, and Alistair Carmichael, a Scotsman bearing the energy of brilliant violet. Michael felt an instant kinship with all of them but especially with Samuel, who emanated a kind of clarity and strength.

"We seem to be a rainbow," Melody commented.

"Verdad, this is truth. I can see it," Sophia uttered quietly. "I never saw such as this."

Melody had set her phone alarm to chime at noon, and with its first ding, an overwhelming sense of electricity filled the atmosphere around them. Michael supposed it had been building since they arrived, but the feeling intensified, and with it the sound of the hum magnified to a level that was a stronger version of what they experienced around the breakfast table. In that moment, the space was bathed in a brilliant blue light as bright as a supernova, and, when it finally diminished, there standing before them was the impossibly tall leader of the archangels in the flesh—or at least what appeared to be solid matter.

Soon other archangels revealed themselves—less tangibly but as clear and obvious as anyone else present—and each stood behind one of the 12 in the group.

Michael instantly acknowledged Metatron looming over Melody, making her appear so tiny in comparison. And somehow he recognized all the others too as if they were his dearest companions whom he had known since before there was time. And, of course, they were.

Almost imperceptibly, Michael said, "How could I have forgotten?"

The great archangel who stood with him replied, "You had to forget, my friend. It was necessary. None of you were meant to know until the time was right for your work to truly begin. And now that time has come."

Metatron continued: "Beloved children of creation's light, you are here on behalf of all of us, for an earthly aspect is required to hold the energies for the shifting of humanity from fear to love." As he spoke, a pure white light filled with swirling rainbow colors surrounded the entire group.

Archangel Michael said, "Outside this circle, all that transpires here is invisible and unheard as I hold you within the heart flame of the Creator of all life."

Michael felt a huge extension of his own heart flames as his namesake spoke and began to sense his inner blue-white fire merging with the archangel's. A circle of that blazing essence enfolded and warmed them all. As Michael gazed around the group, each person followed suit. It was effortless and natural. Tomiko's pink glow united with Archangel Chamuel's; Yas' white flame merged into Gabriel's; Anaishe's magenta fire joined with Ariel's; the emerald light emanating from Grace fused with Raphael—each one became a perfect representation of the rainbow spectrum. Michel wore the ruby and gold of Uriel. Aasmi emanated her yellow fire in oneness with Jophiel while her husband Baiju radiated the same pure gold as Archangel Nathaniel. Alastair's violet-purple integrated into Zadkiel's. Similarly, Melody was joining her mind and spirit energy with Metatron, and Sophia expanded her peach light in oneness with Archangel Sandalphon. Their airier energy fueled and bonded to all of the sacred flames and ignited a kind of vortex of rotating rainbow light.

"You stand with us in oneness now—as ever it has been and ever it shall be. This moment is recorded into the very fiber and foundation of your beings, dear kindred," Archangel Michael said. "Each of you chose to come to earth to hold the resonance of your radiant light for all others who share the same expression of the Godhead. In all, you number 144,000; you, beloved 12, represent the 12,000 of your kindred who are in perfect alignment with you."

"None of you must falter, for you are the embodiment of the Creator's radiance, which is sorely needed now upon the earth," added Metatron. His voice boomed inside the circle with the intensity of thunder.

"Feel the love that we are. Be the love that you are." Archangel Michael's words echoed in their hearts. "You see, my friends, love in its purest essence is your only weapon—all that is ever needed to dissolve fear in its many forms and allow life to become the most perfect expression of the Creator's vision. But it must be love without limit or judgment, without constraint or condition. You were born to that kind of love. It is your shield and your sword. It is your purpose and your life substance. Remember that as your reality."

As the keeper of the blue flame spoke, Michael allowed these truths to sink into every particle of his being. His body, mind, soul and spirit had waited for this awakening. Now the electricity of the moment, the full extent of his emergence and his mission, vibrated through him. He sensed the same in all his companions in this sacred place atop the tor. And he knew that nothing was more important than this.

He couldn't tear his gaze from Archangel Michael. Should a meteor drop from the sky right beside him, he felt with certainty nothing could so capture his awareness in this moment as his reason for being here. Every part of him screamed the question, "What must I do? How may I fulfill my duty?" He could hear this thought reverberating through the minds of all the others present as well.

"Yes, my friend," said Archangel Michael, "it is in our nature to 'do,' for we are the *warriors* of the Father flame. But at the deepest level, your role is more fully about *being* and *holding* the light as you stand in oneness with your kindred. Your fire ignites the purpose and passion within all. But you must guard yourself against the traps of duality, for in this world it is paramount to see beyond your differences and regard the truth of the spirit in order to evoke its presence."

As Michael gazed over at Tomiko, he saw her becoming completely one with the beautiful being whose wings of rose flame wrapped her in warmth. "*Pink loves*," said Chamuel in the sweetest tone imaginable. "Give from your heart to every soul you meet. There will always be enough."

Alistair's companion said, "*Violet transmutes and transcends*. You are the essence of forgiveness and mercy. In your presence, all fear melts into love."

Ariel whispered to Anaishe, "*You are harmony—love and mercy made one.* As you abide in serenity, so all around you may live that blessing."

Gabriel spoke to Yas. "*Purity, resurrection, and creation live in you*, my kinsman. You are called to reawaken and rebuild your nation to hold the cause of enlightenment for all. Let your heart renew itself in the purity of this freshly-fallen snow, and prepare yourself to walk the walk that shall lift you beyond conflict."

One by one, each of the 12 archangels offered an expression of their brilliant light through tones converted into words by the inner awareness of all 12 who had gathered upon the tor. After the purpose they carried within them was fully ignited, the sound began to shift, to become a harmonic, a symphony of wonder that seemed to stretch itself to infinity. Michael saw himself through dimensions so far beyond this one that no words could describe them. He was light—nothing else. He lost touch with his surroundings and gave himself to the vision unfolding beyond the sensory world. He knew each of his companions, both angelic and human, experienced this overwhelming scene so fully that forever seemed too short a span to capture that awareness. And the love he felt eclipsed even the images he experienced. He was conscious on some level that in his human form tears were streaming from the overflow of blissful reunion. He witnessed the beauty of all life throughout the Cosmos and on the earth. And it was perfect.

At last, he felt himself being drawn back to the present—Melody's hand in his, Archangel Michael standing with him, the company of companions from eons past and future encircled in light and love upon the tor.

"Now you have beheld the perfection of what this world can be once humanity lets go of the shadow within them," Archangel Michael said. "This and nothing less is your goal, my friends. The program of light already has been set in motion, and you see in the world the result of this. The shadow stirs and fights, for its time is ending.

"Free will is sacrosanct," Archangel Michael continued. "We cannot intervene beyond the bounds of divine law. This is why you have been sent—each with unique gifts built into the fiber and foundation of your beings—in order to sway things toward the true light once again.

"Over the coming period, your contact with us will deepen and increase, and you will come to understand your mission more fully. This gathering begins your truest work, and we stand ever with you through each step forward on your path, yet you must be the ones to carve that path and to choose it in each moment with the fullness of your human aspect."

Michael felt his body straighten as if he were somehow standing taller than he ever had. Even his physical form was ready for this moment, he thought.

"Yes, all of you are ready," Archangel Michael said. "Be comforted in that knowledge, for you were made for this moment, and the Creator of all lives in your hearts—always."

With those words, the appearance of the blue light, along with each of the others in their rainbow of perfection, began to dissipate as the archangels themselves vanished from view. But Michael knew they remained close at hand.

It was a long while before anyone spoke. It took time for Michael to reclaim his sense of human physical existence and ground himself. He felt sure the same was true for the others. At last it was Yas who broke the silence.

"My grandfather used to tell me I was born to do something big, but this…. Gabriel's words are seared into me. *Reawaken and rebuild your nation.* I guess all I can do is let it come to me as I walk this path."

Melody said, "I can see it, Yas. You are made for this job and no one else can do it like you. Trust that."

He beamed in the sunlight of her words. "I will," he said.

Michael gazed into Melody's eyes. "I think I know what one of your gifts is. The light in your words is like that in your paintings. You spark the grace and knowing in others." She smiled and he could feel his statement washing through her.

"Have you noticed," Aasmi asked, "that the circle is still warm? Logically I know the cold is all around us, but I can feel only the sunlight from above."

Everyone nodded.

Samuel, still emanating a clear aqua energy, said, "I wish I never had to leave this place. I have never felt so strong a sense of family."

Sophia nodded. "Sí, es verdad. Ustedes sois mi familia. You are my family. I feel this is deepest truth."

Tears began to fall down Anaishe's cheeks. "Since my mother died, I have not known this kind of love. I felt so alone—until now. I am so grateful."

Aasmi reached out to comfort her new friend, embracing her gently in a glow that seemed as warming to the heart as the sunlight felt to their bodies.

"This world has been hard for me," Tomiko whispered. "I wanted to leave it so many times. But now… I finally feel *home* here in my heart. You don't know what that means to me."

"I think we understand, bella. I love my own family but I cherish each one of you as strongly," Michel said. He took Tomiko's hand and smiled at her.

Michael reached out his blue heart flame to strengthen all of them. He had done this with Melody many times, but holding so many in his inner light was new yet ever so familiar. He sensed immediately when Melody joined him, adding her soft white light to fuel and balance the flames.

The members of their circle of 12 quickly became enveloped, and each one appeared to shift to a centered state of peace and serenity.

"You're so much like him," Baiju said. "His strength and power. It's almost like Archangel Michael is still here."

"He is," Michael said. "He's always watching over us, I think. And I'm no different from you. I just carry that particular signature of energy just like Yas shares Gabriel's and Grace carries Raphael's and all the rest of you shine the light of your own spirit's birth. It's all love. It's just the love I hold is mixed with strength, courage, and power while Tomiko's is the very essence of love itself, Aasmi's is love with joy and wisdom, and yours, Baiju, is pure grace. Each one of us expresses a piece in the puzzle. At least if I'm understanding things."

"I get you, bro," Yas said. "But your piece is pretty awesome, you know. It's intense. Helped me feel like I could tackle the world."

Michael grinned. But he knew he couldn't let their words go to his head. It wasn't about him. It never had been. In his heart, he generated all the love and gratitude he could for the Creator who gave him this gift.

Michael noticed that Alastair had remained quiet, but something profound was happening inside him. He looked like he might burst at any second.

Looking at Sophia, Alastair said, "Hablo tu lengua." To Samuel, he added, "E o seu," and he proceeded to say the same to all who spoke a different language from his own. "I feel like I've gone mental! I seem to suddenly know a lot of languages. I guess I shouldn't be so gobsmacked, but this is *amazing*. My head is filled with things I never knew or at least never knew that I knew."

Melody appeared to be staring into and through Alastair. Wearing that familiar, faraway gaze that Michael had come to appreciate, she said, "It's a gift of your violet flame. You are the universal translator of the group." She grinned at the words that flowed from her as though someone else had spoken them. "Wow, that's a great gift!"

"Well, if I didn't know better, I'd think I was off me head or completely blootered, but I have nae had a drink and I'm feeling saner than I ever have—for what that's worth," Alistair said.

A chuckle erupted in the group, and everyone felt a welcome sense of humanness filter back into their awareness.

The 12 of them remained on the tor alone within their personal patch of sunlight amidst an overcast sky for hours. They stood as long as they could until finally they sat in a circle. The light flowed between them in arcing hues that waxed and waned as each of them expressed his or her truths. Finally, sitting hand in hand, one at a time they shared from within the knowing of their lives. Michael went first and it was his own inner flame that conveyed his essence, his desires, memories, his *story*, in a short span to all the others.

By late afternoon when Melody, the last of the 12 to share, wound up her contribution, the wind outside their group whipped and snow flurries diminished the view.

"We need to get back," she said. "It's almost dark."

Even the sound of her voice when making some passing remark filled Michael with a sense of profound love, expanding his perception of what it meant to love completely. He held his breath for a moment in recognition of this.

Before departing, they made certain that everyone knew where the others were staying. Those who were not at Tordown had all been guided to Segen House, another B & B near the tor. Its atmosphere sounded similar to the place each in the original group had chosen. Michael knew they all had been led to these particular lodgings so they could be close to one another.

"Mel and I have to leave in a couple more days to go back home to L.A. It would be great to spend as much time together as possible before that. Can we meet tomorrow for a late lunch at Rainbow's End Café?"

All agreed. The plan was to spend the day together, perhaps revisiting the tor, and then arrange to book the lounge at Tordown for the evening. Michael hadn't imagined they would need to reserve the entire lounge when he read that was an option, but he was glad now that this might be possible. Since all the rooms at the inn were taken by those in this group, it seemed likely they wouldn't have any difficulty booking the space.

Reluctantly, the 12 of them left their circle of warmth and made their way through the bitter conditions down the tor and back to the two inns that housed them. The last thing the group staying at the Tordown wanted was to go out again in search of dinner, and, having skipped lunch, Michael and the others found themselves suddenly famished. As they walked through the entry door, the aroma of fresh-baked bread wafted through the air.

Cheryl appeared from the back wearing an apron over her clothes and a broad smile. "My dears, it's dark out and these conditions aren't exactly welcoming. Where on earth have you lot been?"

Michael opened his mouth and then closed it again unsure what to say.

"Never mind that. You're all back now and all together just like you left. I had the strongest idea that I should break my policy and make everyone a light supper in addition to breakfast today, so, if you haven't eaten, come on into the dining room and warm yourselves while I get something on the table for you."

"I've never been so grateful for something to eat in my life," Melody said.

"It is the same for me," said Anaishe. "I am too hungry."

They found the tables still together in the dining room just as they left them but spotless, of course. After everyone took their seats, Cheryl returned with bowls of hot veggie soup, dinner rolls, and butter. Soon everyone had a meal in front of them, and they quickly remembered how pleasant this part of being human was.

"This soup tastes like it was prepared by an angel," Michael said when Cheryl returned to bring another dish.

"Well, aren't you the sweetest? Here's a little bubble and squeak for you as well. It's just some leftover veggies and potatoes fried up 'til browned. I hope you like it."

"We've loved everything else you've made, so I'm sure we will," Melody said. "Thank you so much for this. We were ever so hungry, and this is just perfect!"

"I think Michael is right," said Baiju. "You are indeed an angel. We thank you."

Everyone shared their gratitude and with it all the love they felt from an afternoon unlike any other until Cheryl began to absolutely glow within the warmth of their words and energies. Michael watched her pink aura expand even as her cheeks took on the same hue.

With his lilting Italian accent, Michel said, "Dear lady, you are the kindest hostess I have ever met."

Everyone at the table enthusiastically dug into the food. Michael let every morsel fill his senses. He thought this could be the best meal he'd ever tasted. But far beyond these typical sensory experiences, he allowed himself to feel the kinship with the others present. As he looked around the table at each of them, still discerning the wonder of their energies, he experienced the most profound gratitude. First, his beloved Melody, so certain in her faith and always filled with a flood of creativity. The others felt like his brothers and sisters in a way even greater than the bonds of blood.

Melody glanced at him with a smile that spoke volumes of understanding. She raised her glass, clinking it gently with her fork.

"To the family of my spirit," she said looking around the table.

"Si, alla mia famiglia," said Michel.

Each of them lifted their glasses and extended their hearts.

"I came a long way to find home," added Yas, his eyes glowing with warmth.

Michael couldn't recall a time when he had felt like he truly belonged on earth. Always there was the sense of not fitting. But now in the flow and exchange of energies around the table, he realized he had let that feeling fall away, replaced by a pervasive knowing that he was one with all of his spirit's kin.

* * *

The snow began to melt as the clouds departed and sunlight returned to flood its warmth into the earth and their hearts. Melody was grateful that clear skies would color their last day in Glastonbury. As she gazed out the window, the light reflecting off the snowy ground made her squint, but she felt joyful to imbibe the brightness.

Standing behind her, Michael wrapped his arms around her waist. The cold air emanating from the window couldn't compete with his inner fire. A blanket of loving heat enfolded her.

"It will be hard to say goodbye to Glastonbury," Michael said softly.

She placed her hands over his. "I've never wanted to stay anywhere so much—except, of course, in the ethers with our archangel friends. I'm really going to miss this town—and the people."

A recognizable voice resounded within her mind. "You may leave this place, but you will remain in communion with your kindred," Metatron said.

Light far stronger than the winter sun washed into her consciousness and permeated her being. Powerfully connected to Michael, she knew he felt it too. And she sensed his great mentor's presence over-lighting him.

"Yes," he said. "I suspected that somehow we would stay in contact. But I still don't understand how that's possible across the distances that will be between us."

"You're hearing what I am, then," Melody said.

"Yes," her beloved's voice echoed through her mind.

It was so easy to hear him now. At times, it seemed as if his thoughts and hers were one, and she had to discern which was whose.

They stood there, holding each other, in the joy of the moment until the archangels receded so they could prepare for the day.

By the time they went downstairs to breakfast, Baiju and Aasmi had arranged for the group to reserve the lounge that night. After eating, the entirety of the inn's guests set out together for another day of adventure.

They decided to visit the Chalice Well again, and, when they entered the grounds, the other four of the 12 were there already. Melody was overjoyed to see Sophia, Samuel, Alistair, and Grace again. All 12 embraced each other as if old friends and family were reuniting after a long absence.

"Aye," Alistair said as he caught the thought that passed swiftly between them. "Family reuniting."

"Alistair," Sophia said. "It is agreeable for you to say that in Spanish, but the others should understand you perhaps too."

"No," Tomiko responded. "He spoke in Japanese. I heard him."

"Well, I heard English," Grace added.

"Did everyone hear Alistair's words in your own language?" Michael said.

All of them nodded and smiled.

"It appears your gifts have grown overnight," Melody said.

Alistair's eyes gleamed a bit more brilliantly, it seemed, as his face took on a slightly ruddier hue.

"Will wonders never cease?" he said in a quieter tone.

"Apparently, they will not," said Michel with a wide grin.

At that moment, they all heard what sounded like distant singing coming from the direction of the Chalice Well. It was the most perfect choir Melody thought she had ever heard—each voice distinct but all flawlessly blended into one. The music drew them magnetically toward it, and they seemed to walk as one—each in step with one another as they entered the gateway to the well.

A world of wonder awaited them there. The three-dimensional snowflake and golden-white star tetrahedron within a sphere of brilliant electric blue again revealed itself to Melody. She knew the others could see it too. The star tetrahedron became infused with all the colors of the rainbow as their group of 12 walked into its midst. Once inside the sphere, all of them perceived the presence of a multitude of angels spanning into the distance—visible yet unseen to anyone outside the sphere.

Tomiko began to sing with them. Then, Sophia joined the chorus. One by one, all of them raised their voices in harmony with this seemingly unending circle of angels who existed beyond this plane.

As she sang, Melody's heart felt lighter with each note of this tune that lived in her memory from before time. The song was everything. She knew its notes so well as she had sung them for eternity, it seemed. Always to the Creator of life, the source of all light. Giving voice to this expression of that pure essence was nothing less than ecstasy. As she gazed around the circle, the light shone vividly, flowing from all her companions, and with each note its brightness grew and expanded as the energies swirled around them.

Surely there is nothing more wondrous than this, she thought. *Let this be forever.*

Metatron descended his endless cascade of white light around her, and his voice intoned, "This is but a reminder, dear one, to sustain you through the time to come. The song of the Creator fills and overflows your heart, for it is your truth. Be one with it no matter what the world reveals to you."

Gradually, the chorus faded from her sight, but Melody realized the song continued and would forever. She began to regain her physical senses again—the coldness of the snowy ground below her, the feeling of Michael's hand in hers, his gloves unable to diminish the warmth he radiated, the sunlight shining on her face, and, perhaps most of all, the feeling of her own heart aglow with such love and peace.

As the vision subsided, everyone stood there looking at one another, their faces bathed in a bliss worthy of one of the Old Masters, perhaps Rubens or Raphael or Paolo Veronese. How she hoped she could etch this sight into her memory and paint them just as she saw them in this moment. Tears brimmed in her eyes, and the others shared that glistening liquid expression of joy too overwhelming to contain.

Michael broke the silence at last. "Thank you for this," he said to the divine and to his fellow companions.

Tomiko's tears fell slowly down her cheeks. "The love," she said. "The love unending."

No one else spoke. The truth was known to them all, and its perfect harmony shared by each one in the circle.

After communing for a long time with the energies of this sacred site, they walked out of the garden wordlessly.

That day they visited several places in town, and everywhere they went they were greeted with unusual kindness. It felt as if every heart had been opened to the light that flowed to them around the Chalice Well. Melody and the others realized they carried that energy with them and touched everyone they encountered with its resonance.

When they returned to the tor, they found other visitors at the site. The experience held none of the miraculous wonders of the preceding day, yet St. Michael's Tower and the hill itself still embodied a powerful sense of the sacred. Melody felt the atoms in her body vibrating at such a pace it seemed she would instantly evaporate. She extended her inner awareness and perceived the same among her companions. The hum inside her began to grow in intensity as well. Her senses seemed to widen and stretch, and she understood they were not alone on that hilltop despite the lack of visible angelic company.

She heard one of the people near the group say, "Do you hear that, Henry? It's just like that loud hum that happened the world over."

"No, Doris, I don't hear anything. And I heard that world hum as well as anyone. But there isn't anything now."

"Yes, there is," said his companion. "It's as loud as it was then. I can't believe you don't hear it."

"Maybe you need to get your ears checked when we get back home, love. There's nothing like that happening now."

The middle-aged woman appeared somewhat exasperated. "I tell you there is," she replied firmly. Her face wore a look of determination.

Then, she closed her eyes and just stood transfixed as though the sound called her into silence. The man with her shrugged and continued his walk around the inside of the ancient tower. But the woman, Doris, stayed where she was, smiling serenely as if rapt in the sound of beautiful music, her salt and pepper hair shifting slightly in the wind.

Melody sensed Michael's tender yet strong energy wrapping itself around her. He looked into her eyes with a gaze that spoke volumes. She was grateful they had found each other, that she wasn't alone like the woman whose companion could not hear what was as clear as the voice of angels.

Even with only a handful of people there with them atop the tor, they knew it was a risky move. But, as one, the group of them went to the center of the tower space beneath the open sky, joined hands and began to sing the song the angels had helped them remember earlier in the day, the refrain of reverence and beauty in homage to the Creator. Their voices joined in perfect harmony just as they had that morning.

Everyone else on the tor stopped in their tracks. Doris opened her eyes and stared at them, awestruck by the sound. Although their eyes looked only into their own circle of 12, they perceived the others as if in oneness with them. Melody knew the middle-aged woman's face was streaked with tears. Her companion stood with his mouth open, tears beginning to glisten in his own eyes.

Light flooded the area, but Melody couldn't tell if it was from the sun, the sound, or the presence of a thousand angels standing with them. The radiance became more intense the longer they sang, and she felt the sunlight growing in her heart and mind, permeating everything. Was she still here on earth, or had she ascended into the heavens? Nothing mattered but this harmony and grace given voice.

Tomiko, Anaishe, Yas, Baiju, Aasmi, Michel, Samuel, Sophia, Alistair, Grace, and beloved Michael, along with her, as one mind perceived the world and loved everyone. They sang to lift all hearts. They sang to shift all minds. For nothing more than the joy of praise, they sang—until as one they knew it was time to cease their chorus.

The other visitors to the tower remained transfixed for a few moments. Then, Doris rushed over to their group. Sobbing, she repeated the words, "Angels. Angels!" She embraced Melody and didn't want to release her. Her body shook as she wept. Melody exuded as much love as she felt the woman could accept, and gradually her crying subsided into a slow, silent stream.

Finally, letting go, she whispered, "Thank you. I never heard anything so beautiful."

Melody took her hand and said softly, "I think perhaps you have. I suspect you used to sing that song before you were born into this world."

A look of comprehension passed over her features.

"Thank you for listening with your heart," said Anaishe.

Doris reached out to hug Anaishe then and went around their circle sharing her appreciation and love with each one. The few others kept at a distance from them, but Melody and those in their group knew they too shared Doris' sentiments.

"My husband Henry is a little less likely to approach others," she said. "But I know he would like to thank you too. I suppose I'd better go back to him now. It was so lovely to meet you. Thank you again."

With that, Doris returned to Henry's side, and they hugged each other tightly. Although she didn't intrude upon their conversation, Melody sensed he was apologizing for doubting her earlier about the hum.

When they left the hillside as the sunlight began to wane, they knew their bond had deepened even further. They planned to share an evening of meditation at the Tordown and say their goodbyes then.

* * *

Moments, Michael thought. *It's all about the moments.* He hadn't imagined he could love Melody more, but, when she opened her heart so effortlessly and embraced the woman on top of the tor, his heart stretched to encompass yet another level of love. It was then when it came to him. Before they said farewell to this perfect place, this haven from the world, he would ask her to marry him.

Of course, he supposed he'd known that would happen since the first time he looked into her loving azure eyes rimmed in deeper blue.

He had no engagement ring—nothing to mark the occasion. But somehow he knew she wouldn't mind waiting for that tangible symbol. There were far more important things, after all. For now, he had to put it out of his mind as much as he could. Otherwise, she would pick up on his thoughts instantly as she so often did.

As they gathered in the lounge that evening, they closed their eyes and extended their awareness, drawing in the pure energies of Spirit. Calm, quiet, and serene, nothing outside them revealed the depth of their connection to each other or to the greater whole beyond this realm.

Their kindred among the archangels came to lend support, but they were meant to share this experience more with each other, to deepen the bond to such an extent that nothing could break it. Michael instinctively knew this was what was designed to happen before they went back to their respective lives.

Archangel Michael spoke within their minds and hearts: "Your gifts are stronger when you come together. Be aware that you do not have to be in close proximity to be as one. As you reach out to one another now, the way is formed, the path is strengthened, and you will never be without your companions on this journey—unless you yourself choose otherwise."

As they sat in a circle, Michael perceived energetic pathways between each of them. At the center of the group, a pure white light formed like the hub of a wagon wheel. All around it, spokes of energy in the colors of the rainbow passed, joining with the inner sphere of luminous white. And a multi-colored outer wheel linked them one to another.

As one of them communicated more prominently, the color of the hub changed to the frequency of that person's true essence. For Grace, an emerald green as pure as the most perfect gemstone colored the inner sphere. Alistair's violet flame was emitted when he expressed himself. Samuel's radiant aquamarine clearly transmitted to all when he took the fore.

Each of them practiced connecting with the others until, by the end of the evening, they had become adept at transferring energy and thoughts. This would make it easier for them to remain linked as they went their separate ways.

Nonetheless, Michael sensed Melody's reluctance to say goodbye to the others.

Sophia said, "I shall miss you so much."

"Aye," Alistair added. "It's one thing to connect across the miles, and I believe we can and will. But this…this closeness. I've never known it with anyone. I cannae say what it will be like after we part, but I had just as soon never leave any of you."

Tomiko and Anaishe had tears in their eyes as surely as Melody, and everyone shared a sense of loss at the idea of not being in each other's company for a long time.

"We may not see each other for a while," Michael said, "but I believe we will be able to stay in close communication, and that's something we have to be thankful for. Let's not get down about leaving."

"You're right, of course," Melody added. "I'll do my best.... Thank you for finding us, beloved friends. Thank the divine for bringing us together. I'm grateful beyond words for this time we've shared and for the next time we meet—wherever and whenever that may be. Until then, we stand together even if far apart."

The tears in her eyes and the feelings she conveyed betrayed her brave words, but Michael was nonetheless glad she said them and knew it made the others feel better. Her words always seemed to do that.

After they said their farewells and the others left, Michael felt spent and yet invigorated at the same time. Working with the archangels had the strange effect of stretching the boundaries to the point of exhaustion while at the same time uplifting the senses to a state of profound exhilaration. It was an odd combination.

They had an opportunity to say goodnight and farewell to the wonderful innkeepers who made their stay so comfortable. Since they would leave before breakfast, this was their final chance to express a proper goodbye to Cheryl and Michael.

"Cheryl, your food was as sublime as your smile," Michael said grinning widely and expanding love. "Both you and

Michael were perfect hosts. Thank you so much for all you did to make our stay joyful."

Melody hugged Cheryl and said, "You truly are an angel," her words imparting a sense of truth and deep appreciation.

After returning to the quiet of their room, the two stood at the window overlooking a moonlit, snow-covered vale of Avalon. He held her much as he had when they began their final day in Glastonbury. The feeling of having Melody in his arms awakened his inner knowing that this was indeed the moment.

"Melody," he whispered, and she turned toward him, her face lit in the warm glow of the bedside table lamp. "You know how much I love you."

"Yes. I feel it every second we're together and much of the time when we're apart. Just as I believe you feel my love for you." She smiled with genuine understanding.

"I don't suppose it will surprise you then, my love." He got down on one knee and kissed her hand. Looking up into her eyes, he said, "Will you do me the honor of becoming my wife and sharing my life?"

With more strength than one would expect from her lithe body, she pulled him up so they stood facing each other. "You know I will," she said. "In my heart, I already have."

His heart flames magnified and encompassed her. Her airy sweetness of spirit blended with his fire, and Michael felt as though they were a blaze of pure love. As he kissed her, he felt sure his heart would explode or he would spontaneously combust from so much emotion. He couldn't say how long that kiss lasted. It seemed as if forever existed in a single moment.

In the morning, they would return home, but tonight they simply held each other as if they were already there.

Chapter Eight

Return amid the Shadows

"They must be vigilant now," the Archangel Michael said.

"If only we could spare them these challenges," Metatron replied.

As the two great archangels gazed down toward the earth, they beheld the gathering shadows. Metatron's airy pure white light expanded to merge into Michael's blue flame, uniting their energies and directing them into the dark clouds below wherever the Creator led them to focus. The signal from Source was instantaneous—the inner knowing of an archangel. Nothing in the universe could alter that.

"The humans express it well, I think," said Metatron. "Darkest before the dawn."

"But, unlike us, they cannot always sense the dawn approaching. Too often they are blinded by the story playing out around them to see what lies beyond." Michael's fire took aim again at a growing cloud of density held in the astral level of the planet below.

"At least the 12 have come together, and the two leaders are bonded to walk as one. Whether it will be enough—"

Metatron replied, "No matter how many potential paths lead them astray, no matter what plague befalls them, we must hold humanity in light and trust The Plan. There is yet hope, my friend."

"Always," Michael replied, his fiery wings outstretched, his sword extending into the thickest area of the murkiness below.

* * *

Their stay in Glastonbury had been a tranquil break from the *real* world. Michael wished he and Melody could have stayed in that cocoon of grace they found across the Atlantic. On their return, it took little time for that precious reprieve from the shadows to evaporate.

He knew Melody could sense them too—in the airports, on the plane, and now back at LAX, where their journey began. For him, it had become more than sensing, however. He was *seeing* far more people overcome by the shadows than when they left, it seemed. He felt almost a suffocating sensation as the two of them rushed as quickly as possible through the terminal. Inwardly, he wanted to shudder, but he kept his composure as he passed by one person, then another and another and another—so many whose energy was colored by an inky substance that dulled the inner senses. And above their heads, something nameless seemed to be attached, entrenching itself into their psyches.

Inside his mind, he heard that familiar voice. "Hold yourself in stillness," said Archangel Michael. "Let your perception be brightened by hers."

Michael began to breathe more consciously with Melody and to bring his awareness to her own. He felt her reach out to him internally and say, "Far beneath all else, there is still the light, my love. We have to remember that."

But somewhere below the surface of her mind, he knew that she too urgently wanted to escape the crowded airport and the whirl of disturbing energies.

When they finally arrived home, the two of them reinvigorated their shields with the help of their angel guardians. Each wall, ceiling, and floor quickly filled with the protective divine flames that spared them the intensity of the world outside their apartment. After all necessary precautions were taken, Michael finally let out a deep sigh—as if he had been holding his breath for the whole trip back from Glastonbury.

Melody reached out her hand and tilted his face toward hers. "Only us now—and our angelic friends." She managed a smile but her eyes revealed a tiredness that he understood all too well.

"I feel like I've been on guard duty for the last 15+ hours."

"I know," she replied. "So do I. But it's more intense for you than for me. I know that too, my beloved protector angel. For me, there is relief in the dream of light that almost constantly floods my psyche when I'm not looking at the world outside. For you, there's only watchfulness. Always on the alert. I don't want your job, my love."

He grinned for what was probably the first time since they left Glastonbury. "Well, it's what I signed up for, after all. And then there's you. If you weren't here, I don't know how I could manage all of this. But with you by my side, I have something more personal to protect. It's one thing to have the whole world to fight for, but with you… Having you here makes all that vigilance mean something."

He didn't want to tell her how much more shadow he sensed on their return trip. But, of course, she knew.

Reading his mind again, she said, "Do you think there really is more, or maybe it just seems that way after having a week of freedom in a place of so much light?"

He paused before answering, hoping she might be right. "No, I'm pretty sure there's more now. There wasn't this much before we left."

For just an instant, he felt frightened, and she picked up on even that fleeting emotion.

"You know what they say, right? Courage isn't the absence of fear; it's having the fear and still facing the thing you're afraid of," she said softly. "I can't remember who said that. Maybe Nelson Mandela. I'm afraid too, you know. But with you beside me and knowing the archangels have our backs, whatever comes I know we'll be all right."

He pulled her to him and held her tightly for a long while. His body started to relax for the first time since they began the long trip home. All those muscles that he hadn't realized were held rigid started to let go as he seemed to melt into her energy there on the couch. *Whatever comes*, he thought, *we'll have each other.*

* * *

Hours had passed while they slept unconscious there in each other's embrace. Michael's neck was stiff when he awakened. He heard the clanging of pots as Melody moved around in the kitchen.

"I could use something to eat about now," he called to her. "But I thought we'd just order some Chinese food."

She entered the room and smiled. "Well, I figured I'd make some soup so we didn't waste the veggies that were still in the fridge. After a week, they may not be the freshest, but at least they'll get eaten. I added some rice noodles and spices, so it may taste a wee bit Asian anyway."

As the soup slowly simmered, they decided to try to reach out to their spirit kindred across the miles. Yas' flight had left a few hours after theirs, so he was likely to be back in New Mexico and was closer than the others, which was the reason they chose him. The two of them linked consciousnesses and called on the archangels. Michael felt so at home when he merged with Melody, and the sense was amplified times one thousand as Archangels Michael and Metatron connected to them.

They envisioned Yas and his pure flame and reached out to him with love from the depths of their hearts. They held the visualization of him dressed as he had been when they departed, emanating and surrounded by a powerful white light. After a few moments, Michael began to sense his faraway friend, and he knew Melody did as well.

They stopped "trying" to reach him and just let go, trusting that the divine would do the rest.

"Yas," Michael said soundlessly. He could see Yas in his mind's eye. He had changed clothes and was relaxing on the couch in his place.

"My brother," Yas spoke within the internal circuitry of the spirit mind. And sister too." Yas smiled transmitting an energy of warmth as he did. "I was just thinking of you. *Go figure*." Laughter echoed like liquid sunlight between them. "Spirit is always at work."

"Mel and I wanted to check in with you. Glad you got back home safely."

"A lot of shadow out there, my friend. But I'm sure you sensed that too," Yas said.

As they connected across the miles, an odd sound interrupted their communication. The whirring noise seemed to grow louder and more intense as if they were surrounded by a tornado.

"Metatron, what's happening?" Melody said.

But it was Archangel Michael who answered. "We are working together to cease the activity of those who seek to access your communication. The blue flame and the whirlwind of white light are shutting them out. When you signal one another across a distance, it is necessary to safeguard your efforts. There are those even now attempting to intrude upon your conversation. This has been thwarted."

Within a few moments, the three of them felt themselves being spiritually lifted, carried high above the earth.

Soon Michael found himself again in that nexus of peace, where he and Melody had experienced such a profound bond with the archangels. And Yas was there with them along with Archangel Gabriel.

"Behold what is happening below, beloved kindred," intoned Archangel Michael.

From this space of ultimate harmony, they could view the chaos of the planet below as if peering from a distance through a telescopic tunnel of light.

"Do not judge what you perceive," Archangel Gabriel said, his white fire of the eternal mind blazing outward to engulf them. "Rather take hope in what is yet light."

Although their bodies were anchored far beneath their current vantage point, the three of them maintained the appearance of their physical forms. Michael gazed at Melody and then at Yas. Their eyes glistened with tears. He had no wish to look toward what they saw but did as instructed. There seemed to be huge pockets of shadow covering parts of the world. Los Angeles appeared to be the darkest spot in all of the West Coast. But there were many others. Michael understood the tears of his companions.

Archangel Michael's voice resounded in their minds. "No!" His voice thundered within them. "We did not show you this to evoke despair. See what is and *imagine* what can be. Rise into what you seek. Do not sink into sorrow, beloved ones. You came to *alter* the tide of shadow, *not* to be swallowed by it. This is most vital."

Michael knew Melody's hand was with her body, but he felt her take hold of his nonetheless here in this place of spirit and light. With great love pouring through her, she said, "I see the limitless potential of what *can* be."

Metatron was enveloping her psyche, his massive white light washing through her. Each of the archangels did the same. And Michael felt buoyed completely by the archangel for whom he was named. He began to sense the legions of light at work around the world—everywhere they were invited to bring assistance and welcomed with a truly open heart.

"Not all hearts are open to us, my friend," Archangel Michael said. "Some who call with great fervor have closed the door on our help by placing their focus so fully upon the shadow that they have become immersed in it, blocking the path of true light."

Michael Browne realized this statement came as an answer to his own thoughts. Why would anyone close that door to help?

"Anger, hatred, blame, self-pity—all such feelings bar the door," Archangel Michael added. "Faith cannot abide in the midst of these emotions. Their very essence precludes the existence of faith. And without that open door of faith, we must stand and wait until each soul is ready to make the leap."

The sound of the rushing wind-like energy began to subside, and Metatron over-lit them with a great influx of calming, creative energy.

"The disturbance has passed, beloved ones," Metatron intoned. "The efforts of those who seek to harm and hinder were foiled once again. Michael and I have taken these measures on your behalf many times without your awareness—thanks to your own open hearts. But today, here in our midst, you were privy to what was occurring."

Yas said, "Is this always happening?"

Gabriel's pure flame flooded them as his reply came. "During this time of shifting realities, diligence is required. We will protect you upon such occasions as long as you let us."

"We asked a great thing of you, our kindred," Archangel Michael added. "While you walk the earth, you must be *aware* yet remain in a state of calm. Do not seek to view or recognize the shadow, for you will always be able to do this; rather seek to remember the light and to live its qualities. If you can do this, our protection is assured."

"Now it is time for you to return to your bodies," Metatron spoke. "We must not keep you here too long."

Michael sensed that his companions shared his thought of not really wanting to go back. If he could, he would gladly stay here. But he knew the three of them were needed in the world below and reluctantly let go of his desire to remain in order to more easily return to the physical.

Back in their bodies, the connection to Yas remained strong. He communicated across the miles, "I'm here if you need me, bro. You too, beautiful song of the heavens."

Melody smiled inner warmth and love, and the three of them allowed their merged mind-heart-spirit link to release.

When he opened his eyes and looked at Melody, her expression soothed his heart and eased his mind. Her light was so strong he felt grounded in the divine heart even here in the world. Her hope engulfed his psyche even as his strength reached out to enfold her.

"This is what love is meant to be, I think," she said aloud at last.

"If only everyone could feel this," he responded.

"Then, we'll have to expand it into the world somehow," she replied. "Because we have enough love to fill the planet."

Her smile, the sunlight of her soul, washed him in that love so completely. He felt as if all the gratitude welling in his heart would overflow to inundate the world.

"Yes, we really do need to share it with the world," he said smiling back.

* * *

Melody returned to work the day after they arrived home. It was a bit of a rude awakening after the trip of a lifetime, but now she at least could carry the love of her spirit kin, of Michael, and of the archangels more fully and deeply into the world.

Everything *seemed* normal enough during her shift that evening, but something felt off. She eyed the customers in the restaurant as she stopped at the drink station to get a fresh pitcher of water. While she definitely had a sense that some of the clientele were under the influence of shadow, she couldn't pick out anyone directing unwelcome energy nor could she detect anyone overly focused on her.

Nonetheless, as she continued to wait on tables, she perceived something strange in the atmosphere around her. Those little blonde hairs on the back of her neck seemed to have a mind of their own and refused to settle into a resting position. She tried to tune in to her inner stillness but kept returning to the sense of uneasiness. She felt it would be somehow dangerous to extend her consciousness too widely to get a reading on the source of her discomfort.

Most of her customers weren't paying attention to her. They went about their conversations as she refilled water glasses or brought or removed dishes. Every person in her station appeared to be harmless. Customers came and went without incident, but the sense of menace remained.

Another member of the wait staff grabbed her attention as she was collecting a tip from one of her tables. When she walked up to him, Derek murmured, "Melody, I just got back from my cigarette break, and I heard the phone in your purse ringing. I wouldn't mention it but it was ringing when I went to get my smokes and then again when I got back, so maybe you should check it."

She knew before going to look at her cell exactly who was calling. Michael was no doubt picking up on her unease from a distance. Perhaps he felt a need for caution as well since he could have chosen to connect to her mind.

When she glanced at the phone, she saw eight missed calls from the man she loved. She hurriedly pressed the number to dial back.

Michael's voice on the other end sounded worried. "What's wrong?" he asked. "Is our former neighbor there?"

"No. There isn't anything unusual happening," she said softly into the phone. "It's just, I don't know, just a feeling."

"I trust your feelings," he said. "I'm on my way there."

"Michael, you really don't have to come. I'm sure everything will be all right." Even as she said the words, the jittery sensation in her stomach told her it would be best to have her fiancé by her side.

She could feel him bolstering her with his innate protective energy. "Okay. I'll be glad to see your face."

"You couldn't really have kept me from coming, you know," he replied.

"I get that," she said trying to laugh off the prickly sense of being watched. "I'll be here."

After a few minutes more of serving her customers, Melody sensed Michael walk into the restaurant. Her back was turned to the door, but his energy was unmistakable, and she had come to recognize it instantly whether he was in close proximity or linking to her across the miles between them. His light felt as near and familiar as her own heartbeat.

She turned around and smiled directly into his eyes, conveying a silent "thank you." Although she still had the definite impression of something being wrong, she felt such relief at his presence.

She couldn't leave early on her first day back from vacation, so Melody motioned for Michael to get seated in her station. She behaved nonchalantly as if he were just another customer, but they began carrying on an internal conversation as soon as she went to take his drink order.

Through their unspoken channels of communication, he let her know that he perceived nothing overtly out of the ordinary but sensed something was definitely *off*. Like her, he couldn't pinpoint the source of the strangeness.

Melody dared not stay at the table too long. Her boss would want her to attend to other customers, of course, but, more importantly, she didn't want to draw unwanted attention. She realized when the two of them came in proximity to one another the light blazed beneath their shields, and she didn't want to draw the notice of those aligned with shadow.

The voice of Metatron resonated softly in her inner awareness. "The vibration of love is the strongest light in existence," he said. "No matter what surrounds you as you walk through the world, know this truth. I am with you."

Her shoulders relaxed and those little hairs on the nape of her neck finally settled a bit. She began to breathe more slowly and consciously, to become aware of the light at the center of all things, including her customers. And the remainder of her shift passed without incident. Her tips actually improved as well since she was expressing herself more genuinely and lovingly with those whom she encountered. *Thank you, Metatron*, she spoke within heart, mind, and spirit.

At the close of her shift, Michael left the restaurant with her—a reassuring arm around her shoulders. He walked her to her car, and she noticed his was parked next to hers.

"I guess it turned out to be a false alarm," she said as she opened the car door. "But it was *really* good to have you here for the rest of my shift."

Michael's eyes were scanning the parking lot as she turned around. "I'm not sure about the false alarm," he uttered softly. "I still don't feel right. Maybe you should ride with me and then we'll come back for your car tomorrow."

"Michael, don't you think you're being a bit hypervigilant again? You'll be right in front of me in your car, after all—unless you prefer to drive behind me."

His smile was lacking genuine happiness. His eyes still looked worried. "Maybe you're right. I can get a little carried away with being on guard, I suppose. But Archangel Michael's presence is really strong right now. He isn't saying anything, but he's definitely *intensely* present."

"Well, that should convince you that all will be well for sure," she said as lightheartedly as possible.

Even in the dim light of the parking lot, she detected a hint of worry etching his brow, yet his eyes still shone with love. She reached out her energies softly infusing his heart and mind with her way of seeing the world.

"Through those rose-colored glasses of love," he whispered. "You, Mel, always see the best in everyone and everything."

He embraced her and let his own light surround her with those fires of security.

Although less than fully convinced, Michael got into his own car and drove ahead of her. He reasoned that if anything was a problem on the path ahead, he would encounter it first.

On the drive home, her eyes weren't looking at the periphery; she was totally focused on the car ahead and on her feelings for the man inside it. In an instant of slow motion, she suddenly saw a flash of steel gray coming toward her from a side street. She felt as if someone else had the wheel and was veering away from the oncoming car. A part of her was watching this as though she could view it all from above. Then, the sound. Metal crashing against metal. Glass breaking. And her body flung forward and back again. Until there was no sound, no feeling. Just stillness.

* * *

The voice within Michael said, "Be calm. Find the stillness. I am here with you."

At that moment, Michael looked into his rearview mirror and saw a dark gray SUV barreling toward Melody's Toyota. He wanted to cry out or to change places, to *do* something. But in the mere instant it took place, he was powerless to act in any significant way. He felt a massive light engulf him and found the means within it to pull over and rush from the car. As adrenaline pumped through his body, he somehow found that core of silence inside his heart. In that moment he had the strength of 10 men.

Michael watched as the other vehicle backed up and somehow managed to speed away despite a badly crushed front end. These things registered on his brain, but he was focused on something more important. Melody. Blood covered half her face, streaming down over one eye. His mind processed the thought that her car was too old to have a side air bag. The front one pinned her limp body in a strange pose.

As Michael pulled open the mangled driver's door, he knew he was not acting alone. There was no way this warped contraption could have been opened, yet here he stood with it suddenly giving way to his yanking motion.

Then there was somebody—someone human—beside him saying, "Have you called 911?"

"No. I…no. Please." His voice sounded thick, strangled. Thankfully, the stranger understood him.

Then, Michael heard the words from the man beside him telling the person on the other end of the line what had happened, where they were, all the things that had to be said. But he just stood there holding Melody's hand and repeating her name over and over again as if doing so would waken her from what clearly must be a nightmare.

"Don't move her," the voice outside him said. "They say not to move her. Do you hear me?"

Michael nodded. He wanted more than anything to pick her up, to take her out of this broken place. Instead, he tried to reach out to her, to the part of her psyche he had touched before—first on the beach and so many times since as their minds, hearts, beings joined.

"Look, buddy, are you okay? The ambulance is on the way. They'll be here soon. Can you *hear* me?"

But the sound was like someone calling from far, far away. Michael couldn't really make out the words. He only wanted to sense her thoughts, her feelings, her *everything.* He tried with all his might, but there was no way.

Michael noticed his cheeks were wet. Like the blood washing down her face. When he touched his own cheek, he expected somehow to see red as his hand came back into view. But the liquid was clear.

"Don't leave me, Melody," he whimpered. "Please don't leave me."

The sirens grew nearer until their sound filled his senses. A man and a woman with a stretcher and equipment rushed to where Michael stood. Gradually, so slowly it was painful, they brought her out and pronounced her pulse thready and weak.

"Are you with her?" someone asked.

"I…we were driving home in separate cars. She was driving behind me. I…I wish I'd been driving in back instead of her."

"Okay, you can come with us. But you've got to be quiet and stay out of our way."

He was ushered into the back of the ambulance. *Quiet*, he thought. No words existed now. He could be beside her. That was all.

Come back to me, Melody. Please come back.

Chapter Nine

Between

Melody lifted into pure light. The embrace of Metatron filled her senses with the feeling of true *life*.

"Child of light." His tone resounded within her spirit. "Welcome home."

Every particle of her being reverberated with the song of the heavens, the hum of the universe. This was where she belonged. Surely there was nothing else. Her time on earth seemed like a dream—without substance or any tangible sense of reality. And now at last she was awakening to the truth of her existence.

"My child," intoned Metatron into her spirit mind. "It is up to you now to choose whether to stay here or to return. This may be only an interlude or a full homecoming. But you must decide."

"Beloved Metatron," she said in the vibrational language she didn't realize she remembered. "Why would I ever wish to go back to *that*?" A vision of pain and shadow played in her mind.

But even as she expressed this, the realization flooded her. The mission was not completed. The role she played might be performed by another, but it was her task, *her* assignment. And there was Michael.

With every fiber of her being, she wanted nothing more than to stay here in this purity and perfection, the bliss of *home*, yet Metatron directed her attention toward the earth, and she could see her body in the ambulance with Michael sitting beside her, tears streaming down his cheeks. She could hear his prayers and pleas for her to stay, and she could feel them as fully as if they were her own.

"Before you make your decision, you must look into the river of potential, the place where all possibilities meet," Metatron intoned.

Her gaze was directed into a seemingly endless stream of fluctuating realities. She watched Michael Browne's world crumble in almost every time stream in which her body died. There were a handful of potential outcomes where he regained his strength and moved forward with his mission—but so few. And she saw both the risks and rewards should she choose to go back. The part of her that was still human shuddered at some of these prospects.

But the answer was clear.

She looked into the luminous face of her mentor, her oldest friend, the one and only Metatron, who was like a father to her. His radiance was so brilliant that no human could gaze long upon it, yet, with her spirit eyes, she could view his dazzling splendor in all its glory.

"How I will miss your light," she said at last. "Will I remember?"

"Yes, this time you will recall every detail of being here, yet you shall know nothing of what you perceived in the river of potential. And you will have no need to miss me, dear one, for I will be watching over you constantly, loving you endlessly, and aiding in your every effort aligned with the Creator. Always."

"May I have a few more moments here?"

"We stand outside time, my young friend, as well you know. We could have an eternity or an instant, and both would be one."

Melody remembered being in existence for more than thirty billion years as humans measured such things. She lived long before time was invented, yet Metatron still called her young. Her spirit smiled at the thought.

Melody extended her light out into the ethers and felt the influx of the pure colors of creation flowing eternally from the source of all life. She bathed in the elixir of creation's heart and renewed her being. To shrink again into a human body would be difficult after this expansion. Even so, she could not resist the desire to feel and breathe the unending light once more and know herself a part of it as fully and completely as ever she had.

After what might have been a moment or an eternity, she drew herself back into the presence of Metatron.

"I Am the light of creation's mind," she intoned. "I am. And somehow I shall live that truth in the broken body that seems so small."

"Go, then, my kindred," said the Archangel Metatron, "for you are needed there. I Am the light of creation's mind, and I shall ever be by your side."

Melody plummeted back into her earthly form. It felt somehow an ill fit, a strange abode for her truer, wider essence to inhabit. And it ached intensely as if a thousand knife points pressed into every inch of her frame. She fought to open her eyes. When she found the strength, her view was that of a hospital room scrubbed clean of any personality with its unnatural light no match for that luminous perfection she had just left. But she felt a hand on hers and looked up into the eyes of Michael Browne. He appeared so tired, she thought.

A gentle and hopeful smile lit his face as he gazed down at her.

"You're back," he whispered hoarsely. A tear welled in the corner of his eye and then washed over its rim and down the cheek of her beloved.

"I prayed so hard," he said. "Harder than ever in my whole life."

"I know," she said. "I heard you. I saw you. You are part of why I came back."

A nurse walked into the room then. "Well, it's nice to see you awake! Your fiancé was so worried about you. He's been by your side night and day since the surgery."

Melody glanced at Michael and sent the thought, "You never left me?" She grinned a little despite the pain. She could feel him showering her with love and the protective essence of his nature.

The nurse called the MD on her case to update him on her awakening, and it wasn't long before he visited to check on his patient. By the time he left, Melody had learned that her spleen was removed, that her ribs, hip and left arm were broken, which she had already surmised from the pain, and that she had been seriously concussed and in a coma for three days.

"You're very lucky to be alive," said the doctor. "Your vitals weren't strong when you were brought in, and we weren't sure if you'd make it through the surgery."

"What about my back," she asked. "I feel some pain in my lower back that's shooting down my leg."

"Compressed discs at L4-L5 and L5-S1 are the likely cause of your sciatic pain. We'll have to explore the possibility of surgery for those down the road. But right now let's focus on healing your more acute issues."

She tried to joke about the pain not being very uh-*cute*, but her silly side was less than enthusiastic at the moment. At least the doctor didn't roll his eyes.

After he left, the nurse injected more pain meds into the IV, and, despite her wish to talk with Michael, Melody couldn't manage to hold her eyes open and soon dropped into a hazy sleep.

* * *

Michael's entire body screamed at him, and it wasn't just from dozing on a recliner since Saturday night. He *felt* it all. The misery she was enduring from the moment she regained consciousness became a part of him. Even now that she was asleep, he still could all too easily fall into those sensations. He realized the medication she had been given was only a mask, some surface cover that could disguise the aching but did nothing to heal the underlying physical distress. He dared not focus on the emotional side of it. But he knew that too was something they would have to face—together.

He was more than a little surprised when she asked him not to contact her family. He hadn't met them yet, but he thought they might be able to join his efforts to help her through her recovery. As he considered her refusal to have him phone her parents, he couldn't help wondering why he had never seen her call or speak to them. But he remembered what Archangel Michael had once told him about the wounds she had suffered in this life and suspected her family was responsible for at least some of them. He trusted that she would tell him when the time was right. For now, he would do whatever was in his own power to support her healing.

An inclination towards vigilance made him fight sleep while she was lying there unprotected. As soon as the thought passed through his mind, he heard a familiar ringing in his ear and the accompanying message, "Unprotected? *Never*. My shield even now encompasses you both. There is far too much shadow in this place to leave you unguarded for an instant. Rest now. I am with you."

Michael allowed himself finally to relax and let down his defenses enough to drift into the deepest sleep he had known in several nights. As he journeyed into the warm embrace of slumber, he found himself accompanied by the great archangel for whom he was named.

They were in a massive room with ceilings that reached into what appeared to be a bank of white clouds with sunlight shining behind them. The walls were lined with blue, white and golden orbs, and the floor gleamed as though light glowed beneath its brilliant sapphire surface. Michael had a strong sense that he'd been there before on countless occasions.

"You have," Archangel Michael said. "You weren't meant to recall most of your visits here. You've been coming since you were a child to this place that stands between the heavens and the earth. It is my training center, where children of the earth and angels of the light have worked together to prepare for this time. In ages past, you have served as a trainer here, but in this lifetime as a human you have become the student, traveling here to remember what your soul knows."

As the archangel spoke through the reverberation of thought and the song of his being, Michael's heart and mind began to open to a flood of experiences. He saw himself in both capacities—as teacher and student—and the training started to awaken within his being as if old memories, long buried, were triggered into conscious awareness.

"This is the natural process whenever you return here," said Archangel Michael. "You will forget again when you leave. However, some of what reawakens while you are here will be retained—only that which you need right now."

The part of Michael that was human gazed at these glorious surroundings in wonder. But as much in awe of this place as he felt, his mind and heart were back in her hospital room, where he slept in that uncomfortable recliner by the bedside of the woman he loved.

"I know," intoned the archangel. His blue flame expanded to fill the space, and the power and majesty of it left Michael feeling small.

"Never small, my friend. That power and majesty is not my own. The Creator lives in all of us. And you and I are surely as brothers. You may speak to me now as you would a brother. I know what lies in your heart and mind."

"Archangel Michael, why did this happen to Melody? How could you *let* it? She's… she's everything that is good and right about the world."

The archangel closed his eyes and allowed his radiant blue light to expand even farther. He did not speak for some time. When his voice sounded within the corridors of Michael's mind, an overwhelming love and peace filled his human senses.

"Do you think I would not have saved her from it could it be done? I cannot explain all the workings of the universal laws to you, old friend. You knew them well before your initiation into the material world of the human dimension. Living in that realm means that such lessons must be embraced through your own spirit as you are ready. Specific laws are in place there that cannot be hindered despite the desire of the heavenly host. Be assured no one in existence short of the Creator has a stronger desire to protect the innocent than I, for this is encoded into my very existence." The archangel fell silent again as the light around him shone ever more brightly.

"Know this," he intoned at last. "The decision to retain human life or to come home to the octaves of light was hers. She chose to continue her mission, but most of all she chose *you*, Michael. You are the reason above all others that she returned to her body."

Michael's heart absorbed this truth and felt the magnitude of it. If he had not been lifted so fully in the immense love of Archangel Michael, he would have wept.

"I was begging her to come back to me," Michael said. "And I was begging God to bring her back."

A circular expansion rather like a vertical tube of blue flame extended from the archangel's heart into Michael's. Warmth and profound acceptance filled him.

"How can I help her when she's in so much pain," he asked. "If I could, I would take it all away from her and into myself. But all I can do is feel it with her."

"My kinsman, do you not see? Feeling it with her is your gift to her. You are not meant to *take* her pain. This is *her* journey. But you will know exactly what she needs and when she requires your aid. You have the gift of all angels who oversee the welfare of humanity, and you will wrap her in your love and in Creator's light, and she will heal much more swiftly as a result—if she so chooses."

"Thank you." It was all Michael could say, but he was emanating that gratitude from his heart so fully that he saw the stream of energy the archangel had sent him turn its tide back from whence it came, now carrying his own love and gratefulness back to the great keeper of the blue flame.

"No thanks are needed between us, my friend, yet I happily receive your gift to me. This is why you came today, in fact, not so that you could give this love and gratitude to me but so that you could remember *how* to do this very thing. This extension from your heart can offer protection, clarity, and a great healing love that flows from the Creator of all life. Your heart must be the vehicle, for the flame that knows no end lives forever there."

Somehow Michael knew the time grew short for him to remain, and before he left there was something more he had to say.

"Forgive me," he said. "I railed at God and at you more than once these last few days before she came out of the coma. I know I should have been focused on love and gratitude that she was alive, but I was so worried and angry that the accident happened. I'm sorry, so very sorry."

"You are always forgiven the moment you seek that gift. You know this truth. You were simply experiencing the range of human response. And I loved you through every moment of it. I always shall. And so shall the Creator."

Michael began to feel a pull as if his body were calling him back down to earth. He wanted profoundly to stay in this space, yet he desired equally to be there watching over her.

"You are always here," said Archangel Michael, "*and* there. Your human expression of life cannot fathom this, yet it is nonetheless true. You, my kinsman, are ever blazing by my side and I by yours. For now, return to the world of illusion, but remember you also remain here in the space beyond time."

Within moments, Michael Browne was back in his body, which protested his waking into the discomfort of his current perch. Nonetheless, he opened his eyes and found hers looking at him, a welcoming and thankful expression shining from them through sleepy lids. Her lips wore a weak yet sincere smile. Yes, he too would choose this world—for her. No matter the wonders that awaited beyond the veil.

* * *

"You were *there*, weren't you?" she said quietly. Her voice was barely audible, but he understood her meaning.

He nodded. He was grateful that no one else was in the hospital room. So often staff seemed to come and go at every hour of the day and night. He was appreciative of their attentions although he wished she could just rest deeply. The door was closed now, and only the sound of her heart monitor beeped its rhythm into the room. Leaning forward, he took her hand again. He knew his heart was beating in time with hers.

"I was with Archangel Michael," he said. "It's hard to come back. But you know that."

Understanding glimmered in her eyes along with the kind of reverence so often depicted on the faces of saints in Renaissance art.

Michael could feel her reaching out to him with her mind and heart. The sensation had become familiar but carried less strength now than the overwhelming oneness they shared before the accident. It was as though a fog existed around her thoughts. He imagined the drugs were responsible.

"Yes," she whispered. "The pain meds are dulling all my senses, but thankfully I can still receive your thoughts through that cloudiness."

So many different people wearing scrubs entered the room that Michael didn't even remove his gaze from Melody when he heard the quiet whoosh of the door opening. But he didn't have to shift his gaze to feel the alarm travel up his spine and a prickling sensation spread across the nape of his neck. At the same moment, the hum returned to his mind and seemed to permeate the space around him. As he turned toward the intruder dressed in the typical hospital uniform, he glimpsed a face he recognized all too well: his neighbor from the apartment complex where they used to live. But more than this, he saw the shadowy figure looming over the man's head and the murky, dark energy that surrounded him reaching out into the room.

"Well, look who it is," said the man, a sneer on his face.

Michael's every muscle tensed as he eyed the man crossing the room and writing his name, Roger, in the slot for the night nurse.

"I'm filling in tonight for your regular nurse. She unfortunately had an accident." Then, gazing pointedly at Melody, he added, "Looks like that's going around." Something about his voice seemed less than human.

Michael could sense Melody's body frozen to the bed. He could feel the turmoil of her emotions that even the heavy pain medication failed to dull.

What do I do? His thoughts rang out as every fiber of his being called to the Archangel Michael. He thought he heard the words, "Be still."

Roger went about doing all the normal nurse's routines. He walked over to the bed and checked Melody's IV bag, which was still half full, looked at the heart monitor for her pulse rate.

"Hmm…a little high, it seems." His expression couldn't really be called a grin. It was some foreign facsimile as though what lay beneath the surface didn't actually know how to smile.

Michael inspected his every motion. He wanted to be sure that nothing the man did would harm Melody. Other than his presence, of course.

"Now that I'm on duty, perhaps you'd like to take a break and go to the cafeteria before it closes," the man said. "After all, surely you can trust your former neighbor to take care of things."

"I'm good," Michael replied. Then, he spoke with emphasis on every word, "I'll be here all night. Just like every night."

"Well," Roger said looking toward Melody, "isn't it nice to have such a devoted fiancé? It appears he's determined not to leave your side." The slightest dissatisfaction was conveyed in his tone.

Melody wisely said nothing. Her outer demeanor appeared calm and slightly sleepy. The latter was probably true given her medication, but Michael knew the former most assuredly was *not*.

"It's almost time for your pain meds," added the man. "I see your next dose is due in just over an hour. I'll be back then unless you need me sooner."

"I won't be needing them," Melody said. "I already feel too out of it to carry on a conversation with the man I love," she said nodding toward Michael. "So I'm going to skip this next dose."

Michael watched Roger's energy reach out to Melody. In truth, he mostly felt it, but he could detect a visible shadow emanating from the man and spilling into the atmosphere around her.

"Really?" he said, his words accompanied by a disbelieving scoff. "That's a first. Most of my patients can hardly wait. We want to stay ahead of the pain, you know. If you get behind too much, well, let's just say things can feel much worse before they feel better again."

"I'll be all right," she said quietly. "I'm definite about this."

"It's your call, of course," said Nurse Roger, coldness in his voice.

He quickly left the room, but the energy, the shadow still pervaded the space.

Michael looked into Melody's eyes, conveying volumes with his gaze even as he put a finger to his lips indicating they might want to remain quiet. He knew he needed to talk to her but sensed that somehow Roger was still listening, not by the ordinary means of an ear to the door but in some way Michael did not grasp just yet.

He tried to reach out to Melody with his mind and heart, but it was like walking through molasses. A thick, viscous energy seemed to fill the space around her. So instead

Michael went inside. He called with his entire being to the great archangel until once again he could feel the intense and powerful presence surrounding him. He knew he had to sink deeper into his true core, his heart, so he dove into that sacred space as he breathed the blue fire of his soul.

"I am with you," Archangel Michael said. "What you are sensing we call dark energy, and, yes, it was left here purposefully. The ones directing this man hope to limit Melody's recovery and to cut her off from the Creator of all light and life. This energy has consciousness and is still connected to the entity that overshadows the one known to you as Roger."

"Can't you get rid of it, Archangel Michael? The energy, I mean."

"I know your meaning always, my friend. Sadly, I cannot—at least not at this time. You see, Melody judged the man as he entered this room, and she feared him, which compounded the judgment. In so doing, she allowed an opening for the energy to connect to her psychically and, because the fear expressed through every cell in her body, also physically. Until the judgment and the fear are released through the doorway of complete forgiveness, this murky essence shall abide."

Michael's heart sank. He felt the truth in the archangel's words as though it were something he had always known. And he recalled how intently he and Melody had been warned about judging anyone in any way.

"Does that mean I can't connect to her anymore?" he said.

"No, I will illumine a path for you both. The gifts you have will continue to function and provide what is needed to assist you both beyond this."

"Both?"

"Your link is so profound that her troubles are your own," said the great archangel.

This came as no real surprise. Michael understood this with every fiber of his being.

Archangel Michael added, "I will place my flame in the way of the dark energy as well so that you and she may converse without the awareness of the shadow entities. But remember your task: Help her to let go of fear and anger—no matter how difficult in her current state. Help her to see that the truth of who she is lies beyond this state."

Michael felt the archangel's presence expanding through the space, filling the atmosphere with his own flame to such an extent that the ooze-like energy that lingered seemed less palpable and dense. When he raised his consciousness from his heart into his head, he discovered the room felt airier.

"Now we can talk," he whispered to Melody, moving his chair closer to her. Although he knew his archangel companion had paved the way for them to speak freely, some part of him felt the need to remain as quiet as possible.

Tears began to caress her cheeks. She spoke slowly, painfully. "It's all right, my love," she whispered hoarsely. "I think I know what he told you. I realized a moment too late that I had judged that man. I just wasn't prepared, you see. With the pain and the drugs, his sudden entrance into this room where I'm supposed to be safe—"

"I know," Michael said. "I understand. Oh, how I wish I could be the one in your place."

"I can't wish that, Michael. Believe me, I wouldn't wish this on anyone—especially not the man I love."

He reached out and touched her face. "I do feel things with you," he said. "I sensed your fear the moment you felt it."

"But it wasn't just the fear, was it? I wish I could undo the judgment. But it's too late...." Her voice trailed off. Finally, she added, "Did Archangel Michael tell you how I could work on getting rid of this *stuff*? It's like being surrounding by some seeping, gnawing, nameless darkness."

"Yes, he told me." He felt like adding that it seemed a near impossible task at the moment. But he held his thoughts in check. He needed to be her strength and hold the highest intentions.

"You have to forgive. Forgive Roger for the shadow he chose to embody and forgive yourself for the judgment. His exact words were, 'Until the judgment and the fear are released through the doorway of complete forgiveness, this darkness shall abide.'"

"Of course," she whispered. "I think I knew that already somewhere hidden deep inside my psyche. But how can I find the strength to do that?"

The pained look on her face as she spoke those words descended into Michael's mind. *Would she be able to muster the strength?* He wasn't sure he could do the same in her place.

"I'll find a way," she said. "I have to."

The last thing he intended was to allow her to read his doubt and concern. He knew he would have to work harder to keep those feelings at bay and allow only light and trust in the divine to enter his thoughts.

* * *

By the time a new nurse came on duty the next morning, Melody's pain was overwhelming. She had somehow managed to pretend she didn't need the medication when Roger checked her several times during the night. Thankfully, Michael's energy and love bolstered her enough to endure those short spans while their former neighbor was in the room. But the rest of the night was filled with tormented attempts at sleep amidst the ever-present pain.

Despite the sensations in her body and the sense that the shadow energies still lingered on the edges of her consciousness, she felt grateful for her beloved Michael's company. She also sensed Metatron was nearby holding his powerful energy around her. As she dozed, from time to time she saw visions of geometric forms in brilliant colors, and something told her these were healing constructs being transmitted by her archangelic mentor.

Michael was reluctant to leave her side, but she convinced him he had to go to work and that she would be all right—perhaps even able to sleep since getting the pain meds. But, after he left, slumber was still a long while coming.

The constant sounds of the hospital screamed into her senses. A tray with liquids for her breakfast arrived, and she couldn't bring herself to taste it.

She decided there was only one thing to do: Go to the quiet place within and connect to the angels. The blurring influence of the drugs and the background of pain and irritating noises made the task much more challenging, but she believed she could find a way past these physical manifestations and enter into the silence. She breathed as deeply as she dared without causing twinges and envisioned being surrounded and filled with the opalescent white light that was her soul's truth. With all her inner strength and as much focus as she could muster, she called to Metatron. After a while, she felt as if a serene blanket covered her. Her inner senses began to open more, and soon she saw him in her mind's eye, encompassing her in a breathtaking iridescent white star tetrahedron. She allowed herself to let go and simply *be* until she was at one with its energy.

Metatron spoke. Despite his immensity, his voice seemed softer and less intense in its resonance.

"For a time," he said, "this is how we will commune with one another. You may enter the heart space within or call me to surround you here. You will be unable to journey out of your body until the work you must do is complete."

"I understand," she replied. "I suspected as much. Can you help me, beloved Metatron?"

"I can hold the light of intention for you. I may see you whole and risen beyond this state of being. I cannot forgive for you, but I can create the framework for you to do what must be done."

Suddenly, the star tetrahedron was filled with violet flame and green light that shifted and spiraled. She watched as the emerald energy moved into the parts of her body that were injured.

"God heals," said Metatron. "Raphael is lending his kind heart light. When you focus on mending and restoring your physical form, remember to say unto the light, 'God has healed. Thank you.' In so doing, you hasten this activity.

"You may discern the violet flame has not yet entered you," Metatron added. "It is waiting. When you are ready to forgive, welcome as much as you can into your heart and mind, your body and being. It may take time, beloved child. But every inkling of forgiveness that you feel will be expanded with this flame. When you are complete in the act of forgiveness, the flames of mercy shall be joined by the sword of Michael and all shadow shall be removed."

She wanted to ask, "How long," but she realized this could shift depending on her own ability to truly forgive. She had the strongest sense that in doing so she would move beyond the desire to judge, which would be the greatest gift she could imagine.

"I saw this in the stream of potential timelines, didn't I?" she said. "I remember now."

"Yes," Metatron intoned in the light language they shared. Reading her thoughts, he added, "Foreknowledge is not possible with these pivotal experiences. Your actions and reactions shape your world. It was necessary for you to forget this until the moment you were ready to recall it.

"Sleep now, dear child of light. Your body will heal as you rest. And we, your kindred, will watch over you as you embrace the balm of slumber."

With that, Metatron's presence departed, but Melody knew he was close by, his energy still expanding through the room and her being. The soothing sound of an angelic lullaby played softly as if in the next room. And she melted into deep sleep.

* * *

It took all Michael Browne's energy to focus at work that day. He felt as if his consciousness existed in two places—one back in that hospital room by her side and the other trying to manage his tasks at the office with some semblance of coherence. He wasn't altogether successful at the latter, but he did the best he could under the circumstances.

Since he wanted to be sure he was there before the night nurse came on duty, Michael skipped dinner and sped to the hospital as soon as the clock allowed. He said a silent prayer that the regular nurse would return tonight.

He arrived well before the shift change to find Melody sleeping quietly. He sat silently watching her face relaxed in slumber. How beautifully angelic she appeared. Surprised she could rest amidst all the sounds of the hospital, he felt deeply thankful to see her out of pain.

As the 7 p.m. shift began, Nurse Jane came in to write her name on the board again. He let out an audible sigh when she walked into the room, and Melody stirred.

The nurse checked her vitals and asked how she was feeling.

"A little better after a long sleep," she replied.

"What's your pain level," Nurse Jane asked.

"Not too bad right now."

"That's good to hear. You won't be due for more medication for a while yet. I see you haven't touched your dinner though."

Melody explained she had slept so soundly that she didn't even realize it was there. Michael looked at the unappetizing tray of liquid foods and wished she could eat something more substantial.

Recalling how odd it was that Nurse Jane had an accident that allowed Roger to sub for her the previous night, Michael took the opportunity to ask about her wellbeing.

"Oh, I'm all right," she said. "Just a few bumps and a very mild case of whiplash. I was mostly just shaken up a bit. Such an odd thing to experience a hit-and-run."

The hairs on the back of Michael's neck stood up.

A moment after she spoke, Jane looked embarrassed. "I'm so sorry," she said, her words directed to Melody. "Yours was a hit-and-run too, wasn't it? There's no comparison, of course."

Melody nodded. "It's all right," she said. "I know how it feels to be shaken by something. That gray SUV just came barreling at me, and everything felt like it was in slow motion."

Nurse Jane appeared stunned by Melody's words. "You say it was a gray SUV. Dark gray?"

"Yes," Michael answered at the same time as his fiancé.

"Well, it's doubtful it would be the same vehicle. I mean the odds are astronomical—that is, unless this person goes around purposely running into the cars of women drivers."

Michael could see that the nurse was trying to convince herself, but he sensed an inner turmoil, a nagging feeling that wasn't likely to pass so nonchalantly. And more than that, he experienced that same impression. He had come to realize that such *coincidences* were often more than they appeared.

After the nurse left the room, Michael pushed his chair closer to Melody's bedside. He closed his eyes and breathed deeply and slowly, extending his inner awareness to make certain the space was still protected. Instantly he felt Archangel Michael's unmistakable presence, his energy ensuring their conversations and her room were safeguarded. The atmosphere seemed lighter when he opened his lids.

Now fully awake, Melody peered intently into his eyes. "You don't suppose it was *him*—Roger?" she asked quietly.

"Him or someone like him," Michael replied. "I feel sick. If you had never come to the place where I used to live, if you'd never been with me…"

Melody interrupted his what ifs, speaking from her heart. "Then, we never would have been on this amazing journey, never would have had a chance to find each other or to fulfill our mission together. Is that really what you'd want?"

"No, of course not. I just wish I could have saved you from this."

She sighed. "I may not be up to completely connecting but I do know that, Michael. I feel that somehow it's part of the journey for us to experience this. Maybe it could have been prevented. But it's hard to imagine me reacting any other way to Roger's sudden entrance into my hospital room. As for the accident…"

"The hit and run," he interjected.

"It's just another domino in a long line of them that began with our meeting. But I wouldn't miss a moment of our time together, which means I have to let the dominos fall and keep moving on the path. As long as you're beside me, I know we won't fail."

Chapter Ten

Family

Melody's sleep was light and thready for the most part. She awakened often, sensing even in her drugged state the energies swirling around her. But tonight she surrendered more deeply into the quiet solace of rest and was joined there by Archangel Metatron.

His white light shimmered into her sleeping consciousness with brilliant yet soft colors that swayed in her mind. She was aware that her body breathed light even as she slept, and she could feel the currents of gentle illumination moving through her being.

"Thank you," she whispered within this resplendent dream.

"Always I am with you," Metatron intoned in the language of light. "And never do I require thanks. Let your song of praise flow to the Creator of all, for it is that love I serve."

Melody felt herself adrift in a beautiful sea of light as if rocked on soothing waves as the distant sound of angelic music played again. Metatron joined the ethereal tune, translating into her consciousness profound understanding.

"Beautiful child," he said. "All your life I have watched over you, and well do I know the reasons you do not wish to invite your earthly family to care for you during this time of healing. Your human father has long been captivated by the shadows of judgment and fear that permeate his dealings with others—even you, the daughter he loves, despite his actions to the contrary. Yet, your beloved Michael grows weary ever holding vigil. Thus, it is time to call upon your *true* family. Even now they wonder at your silence in the circle of light."

Melody looked around her in the dreamscape and saw a circle forming—Yas, Aasmi and Baiju, Tomiko, Michel, Anaishe, Grace, Alistair, Sophia, Samuel, and, of course, Michael—all looking much as they did when they found each other that snowy day on Glastonbury Tor. The light shone down on them and their faces gleamed in the joy of that moment. She sensed them reaching out to her now, their caring energies encompassing her from afar. Her heart wanted to extend equal love back to them, but she knew the dissonant ooze-like energy remained outside her shielded area and wondered if she still could reach them.

"I will carry your love to them," Metatron said. "I shall hold the channel open for that which is light."

And so her heart reverberated with the chord of love that was her soul's truth. She sang creation's song of pure light and let her voice join all the kindred in existence throughout the universe.

When she awakened, the tune still echoed inside her mind and a smile touched the corners of her lips.

Michael was there lying on a cushioned bench near the window. He was so connected to her that he stirred the moment her eyes opened. She smiled more broadly as she gazed at him. His face wore that half-dreaming, mesmerized expression that came so often after contact with the angelic realm. He rose slowly and took two wide steps to the chair by the bed.

"I got to share your dream," he said softly. "It was beautiful. I'm grateful for the reminder from Metatron. I don't know why I didn't think of calling on our friends so far away to send their light to help you get through this. I'm going to send a message to all of them right away."

"I think you'll find that they already know," Melody replied.

"No doubt you're right, but humor my *human* side, okay?" He grinned.

The pain in her body started to filter through the aftereffect of the dream and the medication. Michael took her hand and began to breathe slowly and rhythmically. She sensed his blue light magnifying as he began to send her strength. Closing her eyes and sinking into the energy, she felt as if a blue flame wrapped itself around her, cascading into her heart and streaming along the energetic corridors of her body into all the places that hurt. For a moment, she was concerned that he was giving away his own life force, but then she recognized the source of the energy flowed from an endless river shining into him and pouring through his loving heart. And so she simply received, allowing her body to embrace this precious gift. The pain began to recede and she fell into sleep again.

* * *

Michael figured the easiest thing to do was to reach out via email, so he sent a group message to all their kindred of light with these simple words: "Someone needs your help. Look into your heart and you'll know who and what to do."

Cryptic, he knew, but he also felt certain that these few words would be enough. Those beautiful souls who felt so much like family would connect to the angels with whom they shared light and understand precisely what to do. He also was aware that their communication required protection, and saying little made that easier.

After Melody received her pain meds and the nurse had checked her readings, Michael sensed he would have time before more interruptions came, so he took the opportunity to commune with Archangel Michael and establish secure ethereal communication channels with those members of the group who might be awake.

Although it was late, he had a strong inclination to reach out to Yas. He found his friend still wakeful.

"Bro, I'm here under the stars waiting to hear from you," Yas relayed through mind, heart, spirit. "Got your message.

I will get on the road in the morning and be there just after nightfall."

"Are you sure you can do that? I didn't mean you had to come all that way."

"Spirit sister needs me there," Yas replied. "There's no way I'm not coming."

Michael's whole body breathed a massive sigh. He felt more at peace than he had since the accident. He would have help, not just from afar but in person—real, tangible support. Waves of gratitude flooded his being, and his heart reached out to Yas with that feeling.

"Bro, I only wish you had called me sooner. I'll sleep under the stars tonight and drink in the cosmos to strengthen me and then see you tomorrow."

"Take care, brother," Michael said.

"Always," Yas replied. Then, their connection ended.

Afterwards, Michael felt spent and decided to wait until the following day to energetically connect to the other nine. When he went back to sleep on the cushioned bench, he rested better than he had in many nights.

* * *

After Tomiko returned from Glastonbury, she felt giddy and incredibly loved. She easily communed with spirit, especially with Archangel Chamuel, who seemed ever present. But lately things had been *off*. And she had been experiencing pains in her body that she couldn't explain. Her lower back, left arm, and her entire left side ached, and she got odd twinges when she tried to breathe deeply.

But she was feeling more than just physical discomfort. She had felt ill at ease for days. Although it was difficult to do with her open heart, she kept alert and watched the people she encountered for signs of anything sinister. She had planned to text Michael Browne since he was the one of her new *family* who was most tuned in to the shadow side of things. She just wasn't sure texting him would be secure, so she kept waiting. Then, the email came. It was 4:44 p.m. when she read his words—too soon to leave work for the day. Despite the alarm going off in her head, all she could do was wait until she left the office.

After she arrived home, the divine protections she had established with the powerful help of the archangels allowed her to finally go deep into the place of peace. She rose along a stream of golden light surrounded by the sweetest pink energy and felt the grace of her kindred and the harmony of home. Archangel Chamuel's heart light welcomed her.

"Daughter of divine love," Chamuel resounded into her mind, heart, and soul. "Your sister of light needs you."

Tomiko saw clearly the vision of what had happened and the picture of Melody in her hospital room and Michael lying on a bench nearby. Wrapped in a degree of love so complete that nothing less than its pure essence could reach her, she was able to view this scene without distress. She simply held love for them.

Chamuel continued, "You must free yourself of her pain, dear one. It is your nature to experience the distress of others and even more keenly when its source is your kindred, yet you cannot assist her by suffering with her."

Tomiko suddenly grasped everything she had been feeling. The pain was meant to be a signal, a form of information, and a means of accessing deep understanding of the situation in order to awaken compassionate love and healing heart light.

"The heart heals once the heart is healed," Chamuel intoned.

She knew the archangels often spoke in riddles and paradoxes. But she discerned the meaning of this strange saying instantly. She had to let go of the feelings of others she had collected—even Melody's. And in the presence of the pure love that was Chamuel, she recognized exactly how she could do this.

"I give the wounds of others and all pain I have taken into my body, mind, and heart to the sacred fame of love at the heart of creation," she said.

She expanded pink flame from her own heart until it encompassed her being. Here in the space between worlds outside of time, she held every moment of her life in those flames. She remembered through her heart every pain belonging to others she had taken into her being and all the wounds she herself had experienced. And all of them became one with the flame of her soul, the light of her existence, until those hurts existed only as love itself—transmuted through the heart.

When at last she descended back down the channel of light into her physical self, she felt completely different. Little things she hadn't even noticed were gone. And the more intense feelings of these last days had disappeared. She felt clean and free and completely herself again. How long had it been since she was like this? She could not recall a single moment in her life when this level of ease had lived in her body. She almost wept to be so free. *Now I will share this with my spirit sister*, she thought.

She paused in a moment of complete love, holding Melody within her heart and knowing she too could be liberated from her wounds. *No matter what it cost*, she determined, *I will make the trip to Los Angeles.*

She whispered, "Chamuel, my friend, please help me find a way to go to her." She had no idea how such a visit could happen. She simply trusted that if she were meant to be there in person she would be.

* * *

Grace had just arrived home after work when her cell dinged. *That's awfully weird*, she thought. She kept the sound on her phone turned off and never got the dings or pings or any other racket that contraption could make. But it wasn't the noise that concerned her. It was the sense of something wrong she felt when she heard it.

Michael's email was brief and mysterious, but a picture flashed through her head as surely as if he had sent a photo attachment: Melody—battered, broken, in pain, in hospital.

As soon as she got the vision, emerald light started to pour out of her hands—and she could *see* it. She had experienced sensations before of her hands pulsing with energy, but this visible sign of the light moving through her was unexpected, and it felt stronger than she ever imagined it could. Her head seemed twice its size, and her heart expanded until she thought it would burst from so much light. A green field of energy formed around her, and she felt a presence that she could identify with ease. Her mentor and friend, beloved Archangel Raphael, was showering her in his emerald fire.

She sensed the great Michael as well, his blue flame outside her being, but Raphael was overwhelmingly *present*.

"Your sister in the light needs your aid," said the archangels, their intonations of thought shattering all the mental chatter of the day. Nothing else mattered in this moment.

"I am here for her," she whispered barely able to get the words past her lips. But she knew it was her heart-mind that actually spoke them.

"We will take you to her now and later and in the eternal moment that is forever," Raphael and Michael intoned.

Suddenly Grace was in two places. There was no way 'round it. That was the only way she could describe what was happening. She was there in her flat and *there* in hospital with a sleeping yet *awake in the light* Michael Browne and a drugged, napping Melody. The green light that had been building in her since the message again expanded, its emerald flame encompassing Melody's body.

Grace saw the shadowy energies that were present, but she discarded any concern about them. They were *nothing*, only the illusion of something tangible. While she reckoned it was not her place to remove them, she knew they would be removed—and soon. For now, she sent that ever-present energy that permeated her universe to Melody, offering its gift of healing. She watched as it moved into broken bones, injured discs, bruised body parts—everywhere there was hurt—and observed how quickly it started to mend them. Then, its perfect flame reached into the wounded psyche, the part of Melody that felt afraid, and eased those fears, strengthened her natural trust and inner truth.

Grace couldn't have said how long this took, but the archangels intoned, "Enough for now." And just as swiftly as she was there and not there, she returned to being in only one place. She looked back down at her cell phone and was stunned to see that no time had elapsed. But she knew it had happened. She still felt a tad displaced. The sense of being in two places took a few minutes to wear off.

"Should I travel to her?" she asked. Even though Raphael had departed, she distinctly heard his message in her mind. "There will be no need. You will be here *and* there when the moment is at hand."

Grace understood now exactly what that meant. She suddenly had a strong desire to eat or to walk on the beach and feel the sand beneath her feet. Her stomach talked her into the former.

After she ate, she sent this reply to Michael Browne. "No worries, mate. I'm on it. SYIS."

She hoped he would get, "See you in spirit," because she had a ripe sense that it would be unwise to say anything more. *Yeah, he'll understand*, she assured herself. *If not, I reckon he has a good archangel friend who will translate it for him.*

* * *

Baiju Gupta got Michael's email while he was on lunch break. He saw that Aasmi was among the recipients as well. In his current location, he could do nothing but go inward for a few moments to get a sense of what the message meant. Amid golden light that seemed brighter than the sun, he saw an image in his mind and knew what must be done. He texted his wife immediately to make certain she had read her email.

"Yes," she sent in reply. "What should we do?"

"We will discuss after I arrive home tonight," he wrote.

Although the R & D networking center was fast-paced and filled with activity, the afternoon seemed to drag by far too slowly. He watched the clock all too often and wished for the day to end.

At last when the workday was done, he made his way as quickly as possible through the bustling streets of New Delhi. Aasmi waited for him at the door, her amber eyes filled with their dancing light that made his heart sing. He never tired of her beauty and grace. But on this occasion, his focus was on what he had seen earlier.

"I have been in prayerful meditation for her since receiving the message," Aasmi said.

"That is good," replied Baiju. "Now let us see what more can be done to assist."

They walked into the central area of the house, the sacred space they used to connect with the archangels. The two of them sat on pallets facing one another and reaffirmed the protective energies surrounding them. Their palms touched as they placed hands together in front of their chests. Her yellow flame and his golden one streamed from their hearts to merge into one—two fires united. In that expanding wall of flame, they rose together to a higher level of existence and entered into the presence of Archangels Jophiel and Nathaniel. In that place between heaven and earth, a kind of window opened on the scene in Los Angeles. The room appeared quiet. It would be the wee hours of the night where Melody and Michael lay sleeping.

The human aspect of Baiju knew that he must avoid anything other than pure compassion. Pity would only hinder the healing. This thought transmitted instantly between the two of them, and they were not certain whether its origin was angelic or their own inner knowing.

"When we are together as one, our thoughts are one," Jophiel sang into their spirit minds."

"We shall reawaken the joy and grace of the light within her," intoned Nathaniel of the golden ray.

"And the innocence of her true nature shall flow forth from her heart," added Jophiel.

Together with their mentors, the couple showered the purest healing light from the golden and yellow fires blended into one. These solar flames reached into the places that were injured and also into the sacred heart of their friend and spirit sister. A sleepy smile touched her lips, and she shifted slightly but did not awaken.

Aasmi and Baiju intoned the song of the pure healing essence, and its signature of light poured into the body, heart, and mind of their sleeping sister. They saw quite clearly the places where the light did not enter, the shadowy energy held at bay by blue flame until such time as it could be relinquished unto the true light. All this became known to them as was the method for such intrusion.

"Your sister in the light carries this experience for all of you among the 12, and, when it is completed, it will translate to each of your kindred," Nathaniel and Jophiel hummed into their spirit minds.

Love welled in Baiju and Aasmi's hearts, minds, and spirits.

After they returned from the world above, the two of them gave thanks and held each other in a most profound embrace, golden and yellow light intermingling in the song of their souls for what seemed hours.

Baiju and Aasmi wished to go to Melody. But he knew it was unlikely he could leave work for another extended trip so soon.

"I will send assurance to Michael and Melody that we will be with them in spirit," he said.

"I believe, my love, that they already know," Aasmi replied.

* * *

At 7:00 in the morning, Alistair Carmichael was well awake. His uncle's print shop opened at 9:00, but he had grown up on a barley farm and never got out of the habit of rising early. Thankfully, he had four brothers who could help their father work the land that had been in their family for generations.

Alistair was in the habit of checking his messages after breakfast, but first he walked outside to breathe deeply for a few moments. It was good to fill his lungs with the bracing air, but it took little time before he was ready to return inside.

He found the puzzling email from Michael Browne near the top of his inbox. Rather than sink into worry, which was his way in the past, he felt thankful there was time enough to meditate before heading to work.

Breathing violet flame had become a part of his routine since his return from Glastonbury, so he began to usher in that innate light as each breath flowed to the next. Quickly his respiration slowed as did his pulse, and he went softly into the silence.

Far brighter than a billion candle flames, Archangel Zadkiel's violet presence enveloped Alistair, offering him safe passage to the higher realm. No more than what seemed an instant later, he was in the space where angels walk.

He couldn't help the fleeting thought: *Will I ever get used to that?*

"Part of you is already more than used to it. It simply will take a span for the human aspect to embrace the ease of the angel self," voiced Archangel Zadkiel.

As Alistair listened to or felt or perhaps simply knew the angelic language spoken into the corridors of his mind, he absorbed the truth in its refrain. Always the archangels sang into his psyche—a tune beyond words.

Alistair had long fancied himself a bit of a singer and had made up tunes and ditties since he was a lad working on the farm. He loved the grand opuses of the great composers from long ago. His mother's family had made certain he got to listen to them all. But nothing he had ever heard came close to this.

As he thought of it, he began to notice other music, to recognize its quality and motion. Here the whole of existence was filled with melodies, it seemed. Tones and tunes rushed past him like radio signals on a hidden highway made of music.

"Each song you hear in passing is the voice of an angel on his or her mission, moving through time and space and yet outside of both in service to the Creator. Were you to hear them all at once, it would be the symphony of the universe, and all things would be revealed within that song."

Archangel Zadkiel's voice perfectly expressed his violet flame, Alistair thought.

"In this moment, I reveal to you why you are here," Zadkiel continued. "Look now into my eyes of violet fire."

Alistair did as he was instructed and Zadkiel's gaze intensified. The archangel's vision perceived all, and Alistair felt himself merging with it as he looked toward the earth and to that small corner of it where Melody and Michael, his soul's family, lay sleeping in a room faraway. He could see through the skin more thoroughly than any X-ray. He observed the broken places and the ones that were only beginning to mend—bones that had been set, discs in shadow, and more. He perceived the oozing dark energy trying to get in and sensed its goal.

Then, they withdrew. Alistair was himself alone, still there peering into the eyes of his oldest friend, the one and only Archangel Zadkiel.

"All shall gather," the archangel said. "Some are needed to anchor the presence of the light in the physical sense and will need to go to Melody. You are needed there, for your flame is the greatest asset to her ability to shift beyond this state. Will you go to her?"

"You know I will," Alistair replied. Every fiber of his being was dedicated to serving the divine.

"Yes, of course, you shall," Zadkiel replied, "for you are my kinsman. The means by which to make this trip will be made known to you swiftly. Return now to the human world. And know I am ever with you."

As quickly as he was raised to the heights, Alistair felt himself being ushered back to his body below. He looked at the clock and saw almost no time had passed. Still, he needed to be getting ready for work. He turned on his favorite music while he shaved and dressed. A feeling of expectation filled his chest, and he breathed deeply to let the excitement ease. He would be going to America. That would be a first.

Later that day, Alistair received a Royal Mail special delivery post from his maternal grandmother. She was the matriarch of her family and a strong presence. She was also the only member of the clan with wealth.

The envelope contained a brief note. "Grandson, I had the strangest dream two nights past. When I awoke, I knew I had to send this. Use it well." Alistair found a check inside for what was to him a large sum.

"Thank you, Gran," he whispered. "And thank you, Zadkiel."

* * *

Anaishe had just put on a pot of coffee at the travel office and sat down at her desk to check her email. She found a few messages from clients but only one that stood apart from the rest. Her eyes were pulled instantly to the sender, Michael Browne. After reading his words, she was not sure what to do next. A customer would be coming soon to finalize plans for his aunt's trip abroad. *Not enough time*, she thought. But then she laughed at herself as she heard her mother's words in her head: "You make time for what is important, daughter." How often she had heard that statement.

Many thoughts passed through her mind about why this was not a good time to go away. Then, she found the quiet place in her heart, the space where she wanted to stay always. The magenta pink and violet light danced into her consciousness and brought everything back to harmony. It was the way now—ever since her trip to Glastonbury. Each day she came into her heart and found Archangel Ariel waiting for her. His sweet and kind teachings helped her be true to herself.

The song of his words resounded in her chest in the place of stillness. "I understand," she said.

She would go to America. She would stand with her spirit sister. She would help her to heal. The arrangements would be in order.

So long she had desired to go to America, yet she had never given herself permission. This time she had a reason. After connecting to the light of her soul and giving thanks, she rose from her heart and came fully awake.

Indeed, there had been time. With five more minutes before her client was due to arrive, she had the strong sense she needed to ask for divine protection. She had spoken with the man only by phone. He had seemed pleasant, yet she recalled how her back had tingled when she hung up the receiver.

The bell rang as the door to the shop opened, and a tall, pale-looking man walked in carrying a briefcase. He smiled widely at her, but Anaishe did not feel friendly energy behind the smile. The thought crossed her mind of a hyena devouring a young nyala. The same shudder moved up her spine.

"I am here to see that my aunt's travel plans are complete and to pick up the paperwork. I do not trust computers," the man said to Anaishe. She thought there was perhaps some emphasis on the last sentence. However, she let the thought pass.

"I have everything for you right here," she said agreeably. Even as alarm bells were clanging in her head, Anaishe managed to sound polite. *Was she in danger? Why did she feel so strange?*

She glanced at the clock on the mint green wall opposite her desk. Her assistant would be in within another 10 minutes. Her shoulders relaxed a little, letting her know they had indeed been held taut and high a moment earlier.

"Do you run this business all by yourself?" the man asked.

"Ah, no. I am grateful to have a capable and kind assistant who will arrive very soon."

"I see," the man said. "Such a lovely woman alone in the world would perhaps be vulnerable. It is good that you have help—in business. Perhaps someday you will find someone to help you in life as well." The man cleared his throat slightly and added, "Forgive me. I simply see you do not wear any rings."

"I am not seeking a husband," she stated emphatically. "I am happy on my own."

"Well, if you ever change your mind, I *am* looking for a wife," he said.

The look in his eye said something different. *A servant perhaps*, she thought, *but not a wife*. She could not identify the other thing she saw in those eyes. She simply tried hard not to give away her fear.

The bell on the door rang once again, and her assistant walked in with a smile on her face. Anaishe's grin in return was heartfelt—perhaps more than it ever had been.

His transaction completed, the man walked curtly out of the travel office. However, before he left, one last gaze from those eyes sent another jolt along Anaishe's spine.

"I am so happy to see you, Margret," she said. "It seems I am going to need you to take over for me once again. I am going to America."

Chapter Eleven

The Healing

All among the remaining 12 received the message. Some would come. Others would join them across the miles, held in the embrace of the archangels.

Yas was the first to arrive. Michael and Melody knew he was there before he walked into the hospital room. That familiar high-pitched hum grew louder the closer he came. Finally, the volume increased to the level it had been when they met in Glastonbury. Within seconds, Yas strode into the room with an air of purpose yet peace—both conveyed through his movement and his presence. He wore a hat over his long dark hair, which was braided now, and his shining brown eyes targeted Michael, then Melody, with a look of knowing.

In three long strides, he crossed the room. Brother to brother, Michael welcomed Yas' embrace.

"I can't tell you what it means to have you here, Yas," he said.

“You don’t have to tell me, bro,” Yas said.

Then, he gently hugged Melody, being careful of her ribs.

Tears streamed down her face but she said nothing. She didn’t need to speak. Her expression and the energy she emanated conveyed everything. Michael felt a sigh wash over her.

“Don’t worry, spirit sister,” Yas said softly. Then, he began to breathe slowly and, under his breath ever so quietly, he chanted words in what Michael supposed was the language of his people. The sound blended into the hum that continued to ring—now more faintly—within them.

Usually there was a lot of activity at this time of the evening, but the thick door blocked much of the noise outside, and, even though someone normally came in about this time, none of the nurses or orderlies entered. As Yas continued to chant, the archangels drew nearer, joining in the intonation of healing. By the time the prayer chant ended, Melody appeared lighter and brighter than she had since the accident.

She took Yas’ hand and whispered, “Thank you, my friend, so very much.”

Michael cherished the smile he saw on her face, because this time it wasn’t coming through a sea of pain. He sensed she genuinely felt more at ease and in comfort than she had in many days.

“I feel so much lighter,” Melody added, the familiar sparkle returning to her eyes.

Michael said, “The shadow energy has retreated. It’s still here but definitely farther out—thanks to Yas’ prayer.”

"I wasn't praying alone, my friend. All the ancestors and the angel kin were with me, and so were you."

Michael felt his archangel namesake's presence powerfully in the room—along with many other kindred of the light—and perceived it was safe to talk openly.

"I've heard from the others," he said. "Everything is set in motion. We'll be having visitors from Japan, Scotland, and Zimbabwe. It's coming together in pretty amazing ways too. Tomiko works for an international company with offices here, and, for the first time *ever*, her boss decided to send her to L.A. on a business trip. What's more, Alistair's grandmother just figured now was a good time to send her grandson some money—more than enough for the trip here!" Michael was almost giddy with joy as he detailed these interesting turns of events.

"When the archangels want something done, they can make things happen fast," Melody said with a grin.

"As long as Great Spirit wills it and *we* don't get in the way," Yas added. "So half of us will be here and half with us in spirit. That feels right."

The date when the healing would take place was set. It would take three days for the other three to arrive. Yas would stay at Michael and Melody's place until then. In four days, after all of them had gotten settled, everyone would gather in Melody's hospital room at 8 p.m. local time. It would be the weekend, so those who were connecting across the miles would be at home in their safe havens and easily able to join them remotely.

* * *

The nearness of Michael and Yas comforted Melody and eased what had been screaming pain. She had opted to take lower dosages of her meds to allow her to be more aware. She had found it almost impossible to accomplish the forgiveness work that needed to be done while in an opiate-induced brain fog, but the pain made that process much more difficult too. Thankfully, since Yas' prayer, things had begun to ease at last, and she was able to move into a more centered space of love and acceptance. In just a few hours, she relinquished so much to the divine.

With Michael on her right and Yas seated to her left, each holding one of her hands, she breathed the pure white light of Source and allowed her life to be held in the embrace of her kindred's energy. The gentle opalescence of her own nature was surrounded by blue-white flames, and she called with her whole heart and soul for the violet fire of forgiveness to help her melt all remnants of judgment, fear, and anger that remained in her body, mind, and being. Together the three of them—along with their archangel companions—directed violet flame through her psyche, her heart, her body, and her entire human framework. As she sensed the shadowy energy trying to escape those cleansing flames, she simply went more fully into love and grace. She was willing to let go of as much as she could in those moments. By 11 p.m., she felt tired but happy, having successfully released almost a third of the energies that had encroached upon her on the night of Nurse Roger's visit.

With a grateful heart, Melody fell asleep as Michael and Yas remained by her side.

* * *

Michael motioned for Yas to come out into the hallway. As Melody slept, they left the room quietly.

"You don't need to stay at the hospital, Yas." Michael pulled a keychain out of his pocket. "Here's the key to our apartment. You can sleep there. I know you must be tired after driving all that way and then being here so late."

"Actually, I feel pretty jazzed, bro. Besides, if you're staying—and I'm guessing you are—what makes you think I shouldn't do the same?" He grinned. "I know you've been working every day and then sleeping on that bench in her room every night. You can't fool me, you know. How about you go home for a change and I'll keep watch here? Makes more sense to me."

"I'm not going to talk you into leaving, am I?" Michael said.

"Nope. I'm guessing we are two of a kind," Yas replied. "I'm pretty stubborn when I set my mind to something."

"Oh, all right. I give up. I'll take the recliner and you can have the bench."

"Hey, it's padded, which is more than I can say for the ground under me last night. So I'm good."

The next morning Yas and Michael grabbed a light takeout breakfast in the hospital cafeteria and brought it back to have while Melody ate her morning meal—such as it was. Then, Michael had to leave for work, but he was thankful and reassured by Yas' presence. Michael knew his friend would watch over his beloved until he returned.

* * *

As Yas kept watch by Melody's bedside that afternoon, reluctantly he nodded off a time or two and found himself walking into the realm of dreams where his grandfather, his dearest family member, sat cross-legged with eyes closed atop a huge boulder. The sun beat down on his bare shoulders, radiating light all around him.

Lids still lightly shut, his grandfather spoke softly, "Hatsóí ashkiígíí, I knew you would come. Here in the silence, I can see your friend whose injured body calls for healing. She is better for your presence."

"Análí, you always could see far with your inner eye," Yas replied.

"There is something more you can do to help her," his grandfather said. "Let her unburden her heart to you. She is one who needs to let go of the long-held secret she carries, the story that lives in her skin. All wounds are connected, hatsóí ashkiígíí. When these recent ones heal, she may free her body of the old wounds that she hides from the world."

"Thank you, análí," Yas whispered, his voice trailing like a plume of smoke as he felt himself being drawn back into wakefulness.

As Yas opened his eyes, he gazed at Melody who was awake and looking back at him.

"Where were you?" she asked quietly. "I felt like you were far away."

"I visited my análí, my grandfather, in a dream. He's a wise elder and a great healer. He advised me to help you."

"You already have, Yas, more than you know. Just your being here makes such a difference."

"Yes, but there's more I need to do, spirit sis. If you're willing to let me."

He looked earnestly into her eyes and saw all the way into her heart. "Will you tell me about the other wounds you carry?"

A tear fell almost immediately down her cheek, spilling over her chin and down her neck.

After a few moments, she asked, "Can you help me lean forward?"

He could see the pain written on her features as she moved and a loud gasp escaped her lips as she raised herself slightly and bent her waist toward her legs. The hospital gown was tied at the neck but gaped open in back as she leaned forward.

"Look quickly," she said, her voice taut with pain. "I can't stay like this for long."

Yas wasn't prepared for what he saw. Thick white scars etched her back in several places.

As soon as he viewed them, he took her arm and eased her back down onto the bed. She was winded from the effort and visibly in pain.

Yas said nothing. Instead, he took Melody's hand in his and, sitting beside her, went inward into the stillness of his true self to call on the messenger archangel to join him.

Within seconds, the unmistakable presence of Gabriel filled the space around him and echoed into his body and mind like a voice traveling through the canyons. The hum of spirit reverberated through him, guiding him into the deepest place of knowing.

There, he saw a little girl cowering from her father, shrinking into a corner as though she wanted to disappear. He felt strong arms pull her up and fling her face down onto a bed. He experienced the lash of the belt again and again across that small back, cutting into young skin, then the buckle, steely cold and heavy, finding its target with a force that would have knocked a grown man off his feet.

Yas could feel himself being drawn into anger by the murky energy that lingered in the hospital room, but he refused to let it claim him. Instead, he chose compassion, pure light, and absolute love. He imagined himself living in that moment, placing his body between the lash and the little girl. He covered and cradled her wounded frame, taking the beating intended for her. With every lashing of the belt, he spoke the words, "I forgive you. I forgive you. I am the one true light forgiving all lost souls."

At last, Archangel Gabriel's voice called him out of the place of wounding. He opened his eyes to see Melody sobbing. Through choking tears, she whispered, "Yas, the brother I never had, you were there with me, protecting me. You don't know what this means to me."

"Your father," he said.

"Yes, he believed children needed to be disciplined—until we bled. I've spent my life trying to hide those scars."

Yas knew that sometimes silence was the best medicine. He would give her the space to speak her truth. Tears continued to flow as she remained mute for a long while.

Finally, the words began to flow. She spoke of years of abuse and beatings from the time she could walk until well into her teens. Always the lash found the unseen places so the world would never know the pain she held.

"I was actually thankful for that. I carried the scabs and scars for such a long time," she said, "hidden, always hidden. I felt so much shame. I believed I deserved those beatings even when they resulted from such small things. Once, I took a piece of candy out of my father's pocket without asking. He noticed it was missing and knew I had a sweet tooth. I got four lashes with the belt for that. I learned to tiptoe through life—until one day I just couldn't do it anymore and walked away."

Yas said nothing. He absorbed the words and purified their energy. This gift he could offer to his spirit sister.

She told the entire story to him, explaining that it was the first time she had shared it with anyone.

"Michael doesn't know," she said. "I imagine one day he may meet my father, and I don't want him to feel hate for anyone. I've been afraid he wouldn't be able to fight that feeling because he loves me so much."

At last, Yas knew he had to speak. "Spirit sis, Michael carries the strength of Creator. He has the power to love even when faced with great challenges. He can handle your truth without falling into fear. Trust him.

"But, before you tell him, we need to do some work on this wound. My grandfather calls these the soul wounds, the kind that cut deep and can be harder to heal. Are you ready?"

He could see her body was still recovering from the stress of leaning forward and the onslaught of emotion. Her breathing remained labored, and he wanted to ease her suffering but knew the drugs the staff gave her would only limit their healing efforts.

"I'm strong too," she said at last. "I can do this."

Yas gently maneuvered one hand under her back behind her heart. With his other hand, he held hers and began to chant one of the healing prayers his grandfather had taught him.

He felt the winged embrace of his great teacher, Gabriel, surrounding him and the presence of his ancestors, who guarded and guided him. He sensed a giant light of soft white opalescence descend around Melody. They would both be held in grace as the healing unfolded.

Visions of the past, a time before he and his spirit sister were born into earthly existence, passed into their joined minds. He saw a boy beaten, bruised, and bloody, barely able to move as his father lingered in a closet doorway before shutting him inside. The boy lay on the wooden floor of the closet alone, whimpering in the dark.

Yas and Melody stood outside time, watching this scene. They were linked in the vision held mightily by Archangel Gabriel.

"My father," she whispered through the mind link. "That boy is my father."

Yas did not expect what happened next. Melody stepped into the vision. She took the little boy into her arms and rocked him. She sang to him a song so loving and filled with peace. Her light shone brighter as her voice reached out to soothe him. At last, her song ceased and she murmured, "It's all right now, Johnny. You're not alone anymore. I carry you with me." The boy's whimpers receded, and he clung to her fiercely. She held him just like a mother holds her wounded baby. "I love you, Johnny," she said. "You're safe now."

Melody touched the small boy's heart, imprinting a glow of soft white light gleaming with pinks, golds, and blues. She kissed his forehead and left another impression of light softly dancing there. Finally, Yas beckoned to her and together they moved back into the present moment.

"I can forgive him now," she said. "I can let all of it go."

"I know," Yas replied simply.

He gently and carefully removed his hand from the back of her heart, pulled her blanket up, and returned to the nearby chair. She would sleep now. No more words were needed. He watched over her, waiting in silence as her body sank into a deeper rest.

* * *

Even at work, Michael Browne was never entirely out of touch with the woman, the angel, he loved. He knew Yas was by her side and was able to focus more fully on his job, but the link between the three of them was palpable and kept drawing his focus again and again back to that hospital room. He sensed Melody's emotions and felt her anguish. He could tell when she had refused her meds in favor of deeper forgiveness work. That afternoon, the connection almost overwhelmed him to the point of leaving work and returning to her side. But, when he checked in with Archangel Michael, he was comforted to hear that Yas was helping her to heal.

"Pain often increases before the great leap into healing," his archangelic friend assured him. "She is making a vital step on the journey. Your brother in the light will know exactly what to do as she moves into this phase of reclaiming her wholeness."

Michael, nonetheless, had difficulty sitting in front of a computer and focusing on anything. Overwhelming emotions seemed to overtake him suddenly along with twinges of discomfort in his ribs and shortness of breath. Even at a distance, he sensed her feelings and longed to hurry to her. He left the office as soon as the second hand clicked onto the hour at 5:00.

When he finally reached her side, Michael found Yas sitting patiently while Melody slept, a serene look on her face. He motioned for Yas to follow him into the corridor.

As soon as the heavy door closed behind them, he said, "What happened today? She looks so peaceful now, but I felt—all kinds of things earlier."

"It's her story to tell. What I can say is that spirit sis had a major release and healing today, bro. Things are lighter now, but we still have a ways to go."

A wave of gratitude washed over Michael, and he reached out and embraced Yas like a long lost sibling. "Thank you, brother," he said. "I knew she was in good hands with you."

"Always, my friend."

Hours passed before Melody awakened, slowly opening her eyes, which Michael thought looked brighter than they had when he left that morning. Her breathing seemed a little easier too, and he wondered if she'd had pain meds.

"I've got a lot to tell you, my love," she said when he sat down on the bed beside her. "There's a part of my life so deeply locked away that even you haven't found it."

He might easily have fallen into the pit of rage if she had shared her story on any other day, but now she spoke with a heart in the process of mending and a soul already certain of her recovery. Every word was so encompassed in a capsule of love that no other feeling could be aroused. So Michael listened with a heart of love and compassion, and the shadows fled from him.

* * *

Tomiko was stunned when her boss told her she would be going to Los Angeles. He said he had planned to send someone with more experience, but he kept feeling that he had to have her make the trip instead. She gave thanks to the divine for making this journey possible.

Tomiko always had loved to travel. She got that from her parents, who had taken her on countless trips throughout her childhood. They had a strong interest in other cultures and thought it was an important part of her education, so each year they went somewhere different.

Although she had no fear of flying even on long trips, she felt a strange unease when she got on the plane that day. It made sense that she would feel a little nervous about handling the job itself—this being the first time her boss had sent her. But that wasn't what she was experiencing.

She looked around the cabin of the plane before takeoff. A baby was crying several rows behind her while his mother tried to quiet him. Otherwise, nothing seemed out of the ordinary, so she settled back into her seat. Still, the prickly feeling on the back of her neck persisted. She decided to ignore it and simply breathed away her apprehension.

Somewhere over the Pacific, she fell asleep and dreamed of Melody, Michael, and Yas. They were working together to help Melody clear the energies that clung to her. She sensed the angels present and felt as if she too were there with them, intoning an ancient prayer held in her soul since before time. She expanded love into every corner of her spirit sister's existence, and so completely did she experience that emotion, that she felt as if she herself *became* love. One with pink flame, she floated on the clouds.

A strong pocket of turbulence awakened her from this sweet reverie. It seemed as if she had been jerked back into her body and into this reality from a far distance. She opened her eyes as the cabin rocked from the unstable air pocket. Within a few seconds, the shaking stilled and the seat belt sign turned off, so she decided it was time to stretch her legs. She felt a little stiff as she rose from her window seat, edged around the person next to her, and headed toward the back of the coach section.

On her way towards the restroom, she noticed the baby—now resting quietly on his mother's chest. She smiled from her heart at the sight and then looked away. But as her gaze shifted, she glimpsed something strange out of the corner of her eye—something dark and formless. She looked back and saw nothing, yet the prickling sensation on her neck had returned—this time stronger than it had been. She ducked into the restroom quickly and shifted the door sign to "occupied." Looking into the mirror, she viewed pale skin outlined with the imprint of the side of the window, which she had leaned against as she slept.

"Archangel Chamuel, I am love," she whispered, "and I call on the Creator's protection. Archangel Michael, be with me now."

Tomiko felt a sudden electricity flow through her—as if the air around her had become filled with currents. She heard a reassuring voice say, "I am," and she detected an electric blue outlining her form. "Be still," said Archangel Michael, "and reveal nothing."

She splashed cold water over her cheeks to refresh herself and then returned to the cabin. As she exited and gazed down the aisle, she perceived things she had never seen before. Along the walls of the plane, a kind of ooze appeared. Only the windows seemed to be spared this energy. But this was not the most unnerving thing she observed. She also discerned something shadowy over the heads of many of the people in the cabin. She closed her eyes to shut out the sight, and, when she opened them again, everything appeared normal—just as it had before.

She walked calmly and quietly back to her seat and pretended to go back to sleep. But instead of drowsing, she dove down into her heart space, the place where love always lived, and there she connected once again to the beloved archangels.

Archangel Michael spoke to her: "What you perceived was the world of illusion—what you call reality. We know the truth—that the shadow and dissonance you saw are without substance or energy unless you give it to them. Therefore, give them *nothing*. So long as you walk the path of divine love and express its light, you shall remain free of such as these."

Tomiko relaxed into her heart and felt one with all the beauty and love of the divine. She would take care to direct her attention to love and give nothing to fear. This was her solemn vow.

Chamuel intoned his purest pink flame in oneness with the fire of her own heart, and his light language conveyed a way they could assist in the moment with easing the shadow reality.

Tomiko felt herself rising in oneness with Chamuel's clear, loving light. Together they expanded a pink flame throughout the whole of the plane and, gradually, even through the entirety of the world. She understood that only those with open hearts would receive this gift. But Chamuel allowed her to view the world through his eyes and observe the massive change that occurred as the pink flame grew and so many welcomed it.

"Even a single moment of pure love can change the world," he said. "Remember this and carry it in your heart, for you, child of love, are a world changer."

When she landed at last at LAX, Tomiko held those words firmly in every particle of her being and walked undisturbed through the flux of energies in the thick atmosphere of the airport.

* * *

Each time another one of the 12 joined them, the hum returned. On the day she arrived, Tomiko had to check in at her company's L.A. office and then at her hotel, but that evening she visited the hospital. Melody's heart blossomed with joy as Tomiko entered the room wearing a bright smile and a pastel pink dress.

"The sound is loud," Tomiko said jiggling her left ear with her fingers. "Now that I am here, maybe it will quiet a little. I have felt you so strongly since I landed. It was hard to concentrate on meeting people at work."

"I sensed you too," Melody replied. "Yas and Michael have gone to grab dinner. I finally convinced them to leave the hospital for a while. But we could tell you were on the way, so they agreed to take a little time for themselves. I expect them back soon."

Tomiko set down her purse and went to sit beside Melody, reaching out to take her hand. "I have been checking on you often," Tomiko whispered. "I am thankful to see you with the blush of life in your cheeks. I have prayed for you with every breath."

Melody felt buoyed instantly by the sweet essence of Tomiko's energy.

"Is it safe to talk?" Tomiko asked gazing quickly around the room.

"Yes, we're well guarded by *you know who*," Melody replied. "*My* Michael sees to the daily prayers with me helping as much as I can. And *the* Michael seems to be here almost constantly. If he's not, he has his angels on duty… I can *feel* them even when I'm not awake."

"Yes," Tomiko whispered. "I too sense the angelic protection. I just realized how safe I feel in this room. I did not detect that as I walked through the rest of the hospital. Outside this room," she said motioning to the closed door, "is like it was on the plane."

"How was the trip?" Melody asked. Her tone conveyed more than the usual mundane meaning behind such a question.

Tomiko went on to detail her experience during the flight from the beauty of offering healing love to Melody as she dozed to the frightening picture she saw as she emerged from the plane's restroom. Melody sensed love pouring through every word Tomiko spoke.

"But you weren't frightened," Melody said, awe in her voice. "You remained peaceful. And you're managing to describe that scene with love. I'd swear I could see pink energy coming out of your mouth as you spoke. You amaze me, Tomiko."

"Our companions of love and light were standing with me," Tomiko responded, smiling. "I felt them so perfectly. I knew I was in no danger, and Archangel Michael told me to remain at peace. So I did."

Melody sighed. She wished she could have managed to do the same when Nurse Roger had come into her room.

"I think I can hear your thought, spirit sister. Please let go of that feeling. Do not judge yourself. It will help you to heal, I think," Tomiko said.

"You're right. That's exactly what I've been working on. It's odd to me that I've always had an easier time forgiving others. Forgiving myself is probably the final piece of this puzzle. I'm getting there. And very soon I'll be free of the energy that lingers here."

Tomiko's sparkling eyes shone with faith. "Yes, you will," she said. "This I know. I think you already have come a long way—even in this last day."

As Tomiko started to share her experience with expanding love to the plane and then the planet, they both began to hear the high-pitched hum again. It grew louder with each passing moment.

Melody gave Tomiko a knowing look, and they closed their eyes. Together they reached out their inner awareness and perceived Michael and Yas as they entered the hospital. As one, they opened their eyes and grinned at each other.

"It will be good to see my brothers of spirit," Tomiko said.

* * *

Later that night accompanied by that same familiar hum, Alistair entered the room still towing his suitcase. His violet-blue eyes rimmed in cobalt appeared tired, but his smile brightened every inch of his face. Despite the lateness of the hour, Melody welcomed the sight of him and she sensed Michael's heart lift as well.

He set the bag down just inside the door and tromped across the room to embrace Michael, who sat in the recliner, and then gave a gentle hug to Melody.

"Ah, lass, it's brilliant to see ye looking so rosy. I expected ye to look…well, a wee bit peely-wally…you know, sickly. But you're as bonnie to behold as ye were when we all met on the tor."

"You certainly have a way with words, Alistair," Melody said with a grin. "I may actually look better than I did a few days ago, but I doubt that you could accurately call me 'bonnie.'"

He turned his gaze towards Michael. "Am I right or am I wrong, ma brother? Does she not seem bonnie to ye?"

"That she does," Michael replied. "But I doubt I could ever see her any other way."

Melody beamed beneath their shower of loving words.

"Are we all here yet?" Alistair asked.

"Anaishe should arrive tomorrow. She'll be the last," Michael said. "Yas and Tomiko are here. Michel, Sophia, Samuel, Grace, and Baiju and Aasmi will join us in spirit."

"Aye, that is what I was told by my friend on high. I feel the presence of all the great angels aroun us even noo."

Melody closed her eyes and followed her inner senses. She could *see* the archangels better this way. A huge column of violet fire engulfed Alistair and spread out into the room, merging with blue flame that surrounded them all and the space. She let herself seek her own truth and found that pure white light infusing her from above as it so often did. The unmistakable energy of Metatron billowed like sails on a windy sea, and her psyche felt lifted by it into a state of ease and harmony.

"Yes," she said quietly. "I know there's more work to be done, but I feel so much lighter with you and *them* here." She pointed upward on the word "them."

When she opened her lids, she saw Alistair with his eyes closed as if listening to an inner song that only he could hear.

"Forgive me. I ken this may seem strange. I hope it's all right with ye."

She was not sure what he had in mind, but she knew it was divinely guided and certainly more than *all right*.

Alistair walked the short distance to her bedside and placed one hand on her heart and the other on her forehead. Then, he began to sing quietly. Melody couldn't pick out any recognizable words, but the tune itself was lilting and beautiful. And she would swear she could detect violet light flowing out of his mouth with every syllable and note just as the pink glow had filtered from Tomiko.

As her head sank more fully into the pillow, she shut her eyes again. In her mind's eye, brilliant violet flames spread into her brain and down her spine. She also sensed the same energy flowing through her heart to all the other parts of her torso including her injured ribs and the area around her missing spleen. The flame was warm and soothing, and, as it flowed through her body, she perceived its healing effects. After a while, she simply drifted in the sea of song and flame, barely awake and ever so serene.

She wasn't sure how much time had passed when she opened her eyes again.

"Wow. Did I fall asleep?" she asked.

Michael was holding her right hand and Alistair grasped her left. Both of them smiled widely.

"Aye, you could say that."

"You definitely looked asleep," Michael added. "You've been out for an hour, so Alistair pulled up a chair and we both just held your hands to keep letting the energy flow. For a while, I thought you might be out for the night. I was just about to tell Alistair to head out to our place for some rest."

"Yes, you really should," Melody said. "After all that time traveling, you need your sleep too. Sorry to nod off on you like that."

"Dinna apologize for that, lass. We were as happy to see you cuddle down into that pillow and rest yerself. Let yer body heal….

"I do feel a wee bit puggled and don't mind the idea of getting some rest myself."

Yas had Melody's key, but Michael had thought to bring his spare one to give to Alistair. They called a taxi and soon Melody was left with Michael alone beside her.

"I wish you would go home to sleep too," she said. "Of course, by now I know it's no use telling you that."

His hand tightened gently on hers. "You know I couldn't sleep at home. Even the comfort of my bed can't entice me away from your side."

"My love, I just see those eyes looking more exhausted by the day. I have to be here. You don't. One night at home would do you a world of good," she said.

"No," he replied with resolve. She could see determination in his blue eyes too. This beautiful man she loved so much definitely had a single-minded streak.

He read her mind, of course. "I'm just not easily swayed away from my duty. I think I come by that naturally.

And before you say something about my word choice, know that you are far beyond *duty*, but being by your side when you need me will always be a requirement *and* a gift greater than any other."

She squeezed his hand in return and nestled into her pillow again, knowing her beloved Michael would be there when she awakened.

* * *

Anaishe was excited to experience the sights and sounds of Los Angeles. Even the airport was a place where she could get lost. There was so much activity. It seemed like a different world to her. But she soon must see her spirit sister, and so she entered one of the waiting taxis and gave the address of the hospital. As she sat in the back seat on the journey, she marveled at the heavy traffic and the sprawling city. The air felt thick to her senses, and the size of this place overwhelmed her. She closed her eyes to shut it out. She sought the inner place of harmony that was usually so simple to find. In the heavy energy of this city, she could discover only a bubbling nervousness that she anxiously tried to still.

I have no need to feel uneasy, she told herself. *I am the serenity of my soul.* She breathed deeply and inwardly repeated this mantra until she began to feel better. *I am the serenity of my soul. I am the serenity of my soul. I am the serenity of my soul.* At last the smiling heart within her increased its gentle magenta light, and she let her thoughts fade into the background. She put the security checks and customs agents and the frenetic energy of LAX behind her and lived in the moment of joyful breathing.

She suspected she was nearing the hospital at last because *the sound* had returned. It was a great reassurance to her. When she arrived at Melody's room, she put her bags aside and embraced the beautiful young woman who was the sister of her soul. Anaishe's eyes brimmed with tears to see her again. Then, she greeted Michael and Yas, her brothers whom she had never known.

"I am so happy to see all of you, my dear friends. I am grateful to God and glad to be here where my heart called me."

"Thank you so much for coming," Melody said, tears also filling her eyes.

"I would not have stayed at home for anything," she replied sincerely. "I am lucky my trusted assistant Margret could take over for me again. She is like a sister to me. It is good to know that my business is in her safe hands. Of most importance, it is good to be here with my dear family—even in this strange city of so many.

"Isn't Harare a big city too?" Michael asked. "We looked it up after meeting you."

"Oh, yes, it is a large city, but it feels like home, and I know it so well that to me it is like a village…. But let us speak of more important things. Are you feeling better?"

Melody explained how much she had improved since Yas' arrival. "Every time one of you gets here, I seem to make progress in my recovery. Each of you shares a unique energy that helps me to heal. For that, I'm eternally grateful."

"But still I feel your pain, my sister. You have much yet to heal. And there is something else. It feels like a leopard lurking and waiting, watching. I sense it all around us."

Michael spoke softly. "Yes, that's part of why we're all coming together here—one way or another. We're going to help Melody release that energy you're sensing."

"Then, take this gift from me," Anaishe said. She walked to the left side of Melody's bed and grasped her hand. Closing her eyes, she began to hum a song that was playing loudly inside her head. She did not recognize this tune, yet she felt its harmony and peace. She began to sense a great wave of reddish-pink welling in her heart like liquid fire. The more she allowed the flow of song and color to fill her senses, the warmer she became. She knew that perspiration beaded on her forehead, yet she understood that she must continue to let the melody and the outpouring from her heart flood through her.

After a span she could not determine, the song faded and she removed her hand.

"Wow," Melody said. "It was sort of like what Alistair did yesterday but completely unique to you, dear Anaishe. I saw the most wonderful flames of ruby-pink-violet dancing all around you, and I heard words repeated in my mind: 'Sister, sister, blazing bright, you are made of purest light. Know that God's own perfect might shall set all again to right.' And I felt so loved and peaceful—and joyful too like I might be able to get up and dance any second. Thank you, Anaishe. Thank you!"

Michael said, "I heard the words too. At first, I thought you were singing them, but, when I looked at your face, I could tell you were just humming, and the voice inside my head just matched your song."

"It was the same for me," Yas added, "my sister in harmony. Part of what I'm here to do is help all of us rise beyond conflict. But you… Your spirit can't even conceive of anything else. You *are* harmony and joy. That's a pretty great gift."

Anaishe smiled. She felt thankful for these words but more grateful that she was able to help her spirit sister. And of this there was no doubt. Her face and eyes were brighter. Anaishe was certain of it.

Michael said, "Melody, my love, you are glowing." Tears overflowed his blue eyes, and Anaishe sensed his heart filling with such love. Her own heart did the same.

"Yas, will you take Anaishe to get settled at our place? I know she needs to rest, and we've all got to be ready for tomorrow night."

Yas nodded and, without question, Anaishe followed him, leaving Michael to guard Melody and keep holding his love for her.

* * *

A stark hospital room is a strange place for healing. The energies outside her room boiled and writhed with the frenzied frequencies of people in pain and others whose turbulent emotions signified extreme stress. No one who was empathic could help sensing these things, but focusing on them did nothing to promote healing. And that's what she had to do now.

The day had arrived for the gathering. Except for a few occasions when he had to leave, Michael remained by her side as usual, and several of their visitors from afar came and went. All of them maintained a state of silence whenever they were present. Plans were already in place and words were unnecessary. This was a time of stillness, prayer, and inner connection to the divine in preparation for joining across the many miles with the absent six and across the dimensions with their kindred in a place far more serene and perfect.

And so she breathed. At the beginning of her meditation, a stab of pain still accompanied every breath. That was nothing new. Broken ribs were literally nothing to sneeze at—unless she wanted sharp pangs. She hadn't realized how much shallower her breathing had become until she focused consciously on inhaling and exhaling more fully.

Gradually, ever so gradually, she began to breathe toward the bottom of her lungs. When the pain increased, she breathed through it with the aid of their divine companions.

Michael reached out his hands and positioned them over her injured ribs. She sensed a flow of energy pouring into the broken places, and with her breath, her every inhale, she called in that light. She beckoned the precious essence of *home* to come to her to infuse her with its soothing, purifying, healing spirit. In her mind's eye, she envisioned the light mending her bones. Breath was its anchor. And so she breathed—until the sensations of pain began to recede and then evaporate.

At last she felt herself shift into a state outside time. She was present in her body. That hadn't changed. But she was more than this shell, and she felt her spirit's light vibrating through her. To Melody, it was as if a thousand angels were singing through her being. The tones that washed through her mind radiated into her physical form to all those injured spaces where her pain once lived. But in these moments, no such reality existed.

"There are far more than 1,000 angels singing, dear one," Metatron's voice rang in her psyche and her soul. "The gathering has begun. In your world where time is measured, it nears the hour of the activity of your blessing, and all your friends in the heavens and on earth will stand with you."

She started to hum along with the intonations that lilted through her brain. Gratitude and love filled her heart and expanded into every particle of her consciousness—or perhaps to the whole world, for the feeling seemed to stretch to infinity.

She wondered if she sang aloud or if the tone played only in her mind. It didn't matter. But soon she knew the answer as her beloved Michael began to join her in his gentle tenor. Before long, another voice joined in their song, and she recognized Yas' distinctive baritone. Then, another and another and another. In such a deep state of meditation, she had been unaware of their entry into the room. Now their energy—each one unique and beautiful—registered within her consciousness. She sensed them standing in a circle, hands joined, around her bed. She felt Michael's hand clasp hers and Yas did the same on her left side.

To Michael's right, Tomiko stood, next to her Alastair, and then Anaishe beside Yas.

Although the outer sound remained subdued, the intonations within grew louder. She heard other voices and recognized them—Grace, Michel, Sophia, Samuel, Aasmi and Baiju. In the visible world, these kindred souls were at home in Australia, Italy, Argentina, Brazil, and India, but their truer selves were present here in this room so far from where their own bodies rested in stillness.

The humming grew to a thunderous pitch. Melody could feel each of the atoms in her body. She sensed the empty space between them and felt the vastness of the quantum cosmos. A flash of electric blue lightning penetrated the void followed by a booming echo of white light so magnificent and pure that it overwhelmed every sense outside itself. An ocean of love filled her being, inundating those empty spaces. Brilliant but soft pink, magenta, and violet flames washed into the particles of her existence and into the vast space between them.

She saw her human self and her higher self. Her body lay on the hospital bed, yes, but the truth of her being was visible in its pure, gentle light on a higher plane, and there, along with her, each one of the other 11, her dearest friends only recently made, encircled her. Every one of them expanded into her embodiment the light of forever in a rainbow array more brilliant than any colors she had witnessed on earth. And behind each of them, over-lighting them, stood the 12 archangels of divine light, holding their kindred in perfect grace.

Looking down from beyond her physical form, Melody saw the shadows, the energies that lingered and now fought to retreat, being encircled in vibrant flames. She looked deeply into her own heart and revealed to herself the fears she had amassed during her lifetime—all the moments when she accepted anything less than the truth of the Creator's absolute, omnipresent perfection and love. She saw those fears instilled by her family, her culture, her world and recognized how hollow fear was—that it was nothing. *No thing*—without substance or energy beyond what she gave it, what each soul lent it.

Soundlessly but with the full voice of her true self, she said to every moment of her entire human existence, "I love you. And I forgive us all."

She meant it to the core of her being—on every level including the most human. It was all just a part of learning to live a mortal life.

"I am one with every moment of my life and I *am* love. I am the law of love and the law of forgiveness. Thank you, Creator most beloved. For this *I am*. And it is done. By the grace given to me, oh beloved light, it is done."

The words were spoken in the language of light as well as in English and all the tongues of the world represented by the circle of 12. The voices of her companions declaring with her in their union of consciousness and light sent waves of flame into every particle of shadow that had surrounded her. And it became light.

Still, the flames did not cease. They continued to expand. Melody wasn't sure how far.

At last she let her awareness shrink once again into her body and opened her eyes for the first time in perhaps hours.

Everyone in the circle smiled at her and she at them, these beautiful souls who were her family. Tears poured down all their cheeks including her own.

They continued to breathe as one in silence. No one dared speak or the moment might evaporate. She peered into Michael's eyes—so blue and such a perfect match to her own—and held his gaze in hers, bathing in the connection they shared. At last she scanned the circle, her gaze lingering on each person as she inwardly focused her grateful heart light and let the feeling of love flood all her senses. When eventually her eyes met Yas' dark, flashing brown ones, she saw there a kind of dancing joy, a lightness of being echoed by his smile.

She still perceived the rainbow of energy around her. The room was filled with those colors—each one emanating from the precious souls who stood around her and from the source of all light that permeated each one of them.

Metatron's voice boomed its resonant tones within her.

"The feeling you have now will remain. Speaking shall not alter this for you and those with you, child of light. For the span of one earth day, you will continue to be held in this frequency so that what has transpired may become complete."

As he spoke in light language, Melody felt as if a wind rushed through her mind. *The song of Metatron*, she thought.

She giggled and watched as a golden yellow light spread out from her lips and along the right side of her body.

"The color of joy," Archangel Metatron intoned. "Feel that now and let its welcome energy heal your being."

Soon the room was filled with laughter as each of her friends joined in its song.

Just then the nurse entered to check her vitals and medication levels.

"Well, it's great to see you laughing," she said to Melody. "But aren't you in pain? Those ribs aren't really ready for much of a chuckle."

Melody smiled. "Actually, my ribs are doing great. Not so much as a twinge."

"That's impossible. There's no way they've healed enough for that yet."

Michael answered her. "I think you'll find my fiancée is a fast healer."

"Well, feeling no pain at this point would be a miracle," the nurse said. "You still have an order for meds, and I see you declined your last dose."

"Yes, I'm really much better," Melody replied. "I promise."

"You don't need anything now?"

"No, I'm fine," Melody added.

"Well, I'll check you again in a couple of hours. If you change your mind before then, just press the call button.

"By the way, visiting hours are over, and, while the hospital isn't strict about such things, it is getting late for such a crowd to be here."

With that, the nurse left. And they continued to fill the atmosphere with laughter until that hospital room was overflowing with as bright a yellow as the most perfect sunlit daisy.

* * *

"My brother, we expanded beyond the boundaries of the task," Archangel Metatron intoned.

"Yes, brother. Many were healed this night. The Creator's blessings overflowed the banks of intention," Archangel Michael replied. "In that hospital, no one shall pass from the earthly shores into the world beyond for some span of human time."

"The human element."

"Yes," Michael acknowledged. "Yet, the prayers of many were answered, and thus it must have been ordained for these others to receive some measure of what flowed unto our kindred. It could never have transpired otherwise."

"Indeed," Metatron sounded.

"For her, for all of them, shall it be enough?" Michael said.

The two of them gazed into the light streams of Creation, into the realm of probability.

"We shall see."

"The gift was great," Michael intoned. "Probability lies in their favor even if only by a small extent."

"And they have us—and each other—to see them through the storms to come," Metatron said solemnly.

"I shall abide with our kindred until the world is filled with light," Michael spoke in a language that would have sounded to any human like a musical progression.

"As shall I. Praise unto Creator for this opportunity."

"Praise unto Creator," Archangel Michael agreed as the full measure of his entire existence across all Creation reached to the heart of Source.

"And so I am in eternal gratitude," they intoned as one.

Chapter Twelve

Steadfastness

Melody hadn't been alone in so many days she couldn't recall. Even when Michael went to work, he made certain she was "covered" by one of their companions. She finally convinced her friends that she would be safe in divine hands as Michael and Yas drove Anaishe, the last overseas visitor to leave, to the airport.

She welcomed having an hour or two to herself after so much time amid company. She loved them dearly and felt immense gratitude for the visit of her spirit kindred from afar. But now that her body and being had been freed of the shadow energy, she held a deep sense of security. She seemed to have returned to the person she was before the accident—perhaps somehow stronger and certainly freer of the past—and she could discern how much her body had recovered during the healing.

Michael had brought her sketch pad and pastels from home, and she gratefully began to draw for the first time in what felt like years. Her fingers weren't as nimble as usual, but she was able to begin to put on paper some of the beauty she experienced during the healing. She knew it would be impossible to really capture what had transpired, but she would do her best, because she had an intense feeling that anyone seeing such a piece would have the chance to welcome at least a part of the healing she had known.

She didn't look up from her drawing when she heard the whoosh of the door opening. Nursing staff members often came and went. But then she sensed the energy encroaching and had the certain knowing of who was present.

"Nurse Roger," she said nonchalantly without raising her eyes.

She didn't have to see him to sense the sneer on his lips.

He spoke in a low voice—almost a whisper. "You didn't really think it would be that *easy*, did you?"

Melody gathered herself in the fullness of her spirit's truth and then raised her head.

"Yes," she said, her demeanor composed—quiet but commanding. "I actually did. And so it is, you see. Just that easy."

Her voice was strong and filled with vitality. She had never heard herself sound so self-assured, so determined yet completely serene. She felt her mighty companions sending a powerful current of archangelic light through her as she continued:

"Because, you see, I am *never* alone. There is only one power in this world—in this universe—and that is always, always with me. I forgot that for a moment, but I remember now—thanks to you."

His face contorted into something less than human. He kept sending the same subtly sentient and sinister energy toward her. Again and again, he tried to surround her, bombard her.

But there was no way in. This time her shield did not falter, for she remained true to her spirit.

"I refuse to judge you for your choice to walk in shadow," she said. "And I will not cringe from what you have become. One day you will know the truth. Until then, I will pray for you."

The peace and stillness of her mind and the calm of her voice surprised her a little. But she remained relaxed in the embrace of her own truth.

The next utterance from Nurse Roger's lips was nothing more than a guttural growl. If words were tangled among the twisted mass of vocalization, she could not discern them. And they didn't matter. He turned from her swiftly and left the room. She knew he would not return to the hospital as long as she remained there.

Archangel Michael's intonations filtered into her mind and heart. "You revealed to him the power of the true light for the first time. He was unable to bear your presence. For one so deeply entrenched in shadow, you were like the sun's rays upon the vampire's skin."

"You must remember this experience, precious child of light," said Metatron. "Translate it to all your kindred upon the earth, for this is the manner in which you engage the shadow. Remain a being of love, unafraid and unfettered by judgment. That is your greatest strength."

Her heart brimmed with immense love and gratitude to her companions of light. And she indeed prayed for Nurse Roger's soul so fully bound to the shadow that engulfed him.

"It is ever his choice," Metatron spoke softly. "Creator ever offers love to each soul in a constant stream."

* * *

Michael, Yas, and Anaishe were on the way to the airport when they were called to vigilance.

"Melody," said Anaishe, urgency making her voice sound taut rather than its usual softness.

Michael drove onto the first exit ramp he could get to and pulled over. "Be calm," he said looking into Anaishe's kind, dark eyes. "I can sense Melody even when we're apart, and she feels…I don't know exactly how to describe it."

"Centered in her strength," Yas responded. "I sense her too."

Michael watched as Anaishe's face relaxed, her normal gentle, composed appearance restored.

"Her spirit is grounded in love and peace," Anaishe said more quietly. "I sense that now."

Michael's own feelings began to settle. Normally, he would be in his head and filled with worry, but something in him had shifted since the 12 of them united in the healing. More than that, though, his connection with Melody had strengthened and he *knew* she was okay. He detected the threat at hand but understood that she was embraced by something far greater than any shadow. That knowing overwhelmed his would-be worries.

The three of them closed their eyes and breathed consciously, taking ownership of the truth of their spirits and their kinship.

"We are with you, Melody," Anaishe whispered.

And they were. Michael linked with his beloved and with Yas and Anaishe. His strength and resolve were hers. Hers were his. All of them held each other in the deliberate intention of spirit.

As Michael went deeper into his heart, he sensed a well of powerful love within Melody. He wanted to get lost in that endless fountain. He somehow realized she always had the strength that flows from the infinite, from the source of all light. Any remnants of doubt his smaller self may have felt dissolved in this ocean of pure, perfect, divine illumination.

His own heart overflowed with love for her as he observed—her vision in oneness with his own—as Nurse Roger, or whatever once was that person, stormed out of her room with a sense of finality.

Michael began to hear the traffic around them again and knew he needed to get back on the road to the airport.

"She'll be fine now," Yas said.

"Yes, my spirit sister is perhaps the strongest of us all," Anaishe added.

All Michael could do was love her. In every moment of every day for as long as he walked on this planet, he would do that with his whole heart.

* * *

Metatron spoke in the language unknown to the world of humanity. "Creator is well pleased with this service."

"And may the source of all life send blessings to each of our kindred that all shall rise into God truth," Michael responded. "Yet, what lies ahead for she who leaves now to return to her earthly home—"

"My brother, may we not celebrate this victory without seeing the bleakness awaiting them? Anaishe was part of Melody's experience and, therefore, knows well how to lift herself beyond the sorrow to come."

"Your voice speaks truth as always, Metatron. As we exist in all moments, let us revel now in this one of great gladness."

Archangel Metatron intoned the frequency of joy in its purest form. Michael, the archangel, joined him and the sound of distant thunder spread across the sky above Los Angeles. A sudden downpour washed the city in gentle, cleansing rain.

End of Book I

About the Author

Diana Henderson's childhood dream was to become a writer. She started writing poetry at age nine and amassed quite a volume by the time she entered her teens. From early childhood on, she envisioned worlds of imagination and created a haven of peace and serenity. In moments alone with nature, she knew her greatest joy and could see the world as it was meant to be: a place where love reigned and everything was beautiful. She never stopped visualizing that world.

Diana's writing background includes a BA degree in English, specialization in writing. After spending a few years teaching English, she used her talents by working as a graphic designer and copywriter, but her love for writing fiction and poetry never waned. On her 60th birthday in 2015, she published her first novel, *Grandfather Poplar.*

Diana works as an editor and writer for Realization Press and Creative Type. She lives with her husband, their two parrots, and their loving rescued dog outside Raleigh, North Carolina.

Ready for the adventure to continue? It is our pleasure to provide a short preview of Book Two.

Learning to See in the Dark

Book Two of
The Michael Saga

Learning to See in the Dark

Chapter One: The One Who Fell

Anaishe drifted in that space between sleeping and waking. As the plane soared high above the clouds, she felt a little closer to Heaven. At the thought, her mother's voice floated into her mind.

"You'll never be closer to Heaven than when you are in prayer," her mother used to say. "But remember always to listen, not just to ask. Give the voice of God a chance to speak to you."

A rose light filled her mind and soothed her heart. She still missed her mother every day. Instead of going into that feeling of loss and grief, she knew she could reach out to the one she held most dear.

Anaishe let her heart flame of pure love grow, feeling its sweetness and cherishing her mother who now lived in that beautiful place beyond this world.

"Amai," she whispered silently. "I wish you were here."

"I am, daughter," she heard. "When you think of me, it is often because I have come to visit you. I am here now."

Even inside her mind, the sound of her mother's voice filled her with comfort and joy.

"Anaishe," her mother continued, "I want you to settle yourself now. Something is happening and you will feel it, but you must remain calm within yourself, daughter."

Inside her mind and heart, she saw her mother embracing her. Even though she was only half awake, or perhaps in a dream, she could feel that touch so familiar and warm. Then, it began to fade and her mother's presence disappeared.

Anaishe longed to stay in this place, to keep her mother close to her. As if from far away, she heard the words, "Whenever you need me, child, I am with you."

She continued to glide just outside of wakefulness. *So quiet here*, she thought. Soon she felt another presence surrounding her. He had become family by now. So soothing was the light of her home far from this reality. As Archangel Ariel flooded her with pink, violet, and magenta light, she experienced nothing but peace.

"Your friend needs you, Anaishe," he intoned. The sound stilled her mind as if her own soul sang to her a lullaby most beautiful.

"You will be tempted to sink into despair," he continued. "Do not. Stay true to your harmony and light even as you feel all else. We will help her now in the way that is needed."

As quickly as walking from one room to another, Anaishe stood in her shop back in Harare. The scene before her would have taken her into horror if not for the presence of her beloved kinsman Ariel. She would have screamed if not for his healing light.